CONTAINER
STORIES

DEREK FISHER

MMXXIV

www.withanxbooks.com
Cover Design by Cris Crude
Layout by Jon Nix
WAX009
ISBN 979-8-9874787-6-9

Praise for **Container**

"Reading Container feels like being stuck inside a luxury elevator that doubles as a trash compactor — bejeweled, carnivalesque, and ultimately crushing. In panoptic yet claustrophobic prose, with whiffs of Lovecraft and Borges, walls of impossible architecture cave in and floods fill the never-ending tunnels. Welcome to Derek Fisher's elegant dream of annihilation."

— David Kuhnlein, author of *Die Closer to Me*

"*Container* is that secret little drawer in the garage where your dad keeps the rat poison, a blowtorch, his rusty switchblade, and some expired pills with the label peeled off. Except now there's a rabid opossum birthing babies in there too. And your dad isn't around to see it because he's wanted for manslaughter."

— Claire Hopple, author of *ECHO CHAMBER*

"The stories in Derek Fisher's grim and gritty *Container* cannot be contained. Everyone, everything is gunning for escape: Characters revolt against the confines of their circumstances, using sex, drugs, violence to push against their claustrophobic realities, their impossible lives. Even narrative structure is cause for rebellion; the form cannot hold. "The walls always felt as if they were edging closer and closer, and soon enough I would be crushed." The result is a riotous powderkeg: explosive, nihilistic, unsettling, these are stories felt in the teeth that will leave you hoping against hope that they'll break free, at least long enough to glimpse "all that dazzling shit out there."

— Sara Lippmann, author of *Jerks*

"With stories ranging from lighthearted gore to the depths of despair, Derek Fisher's new collection establishes his skill with a sentence. As he did in *Night Life*, Derek continues to evoke a brooding emotional atmosphere that here appears more vulnerable, a little closer to the heart. I will continue to follow his work as long as he continues to grace us with it."

— Charlene Elsby, author of *The Devil Thinks I'm Pretty* and *Violent Faculties*

"I imagine Derek Fisher's brain as a blackened tributary, fractured, seeping out in each direction, where the sacred, mundane, absurd, and horrific each find themselves a stream. His collection defies categorization, except that most every story ends in gnawing uncertainty."

— Christopher Zeischegg, author of *The Magician*

"Derek Fisher's debut collection of stories, *Container*, is an absolute treasure trove of brilliant writing and ideas, realised to their fullest potential. Fisher's writing is a total gift and pleasure to read – he creates mysterious, shadowy tales involving characters who are confused and confusing. The atmosphere is tense at times and darkly funny at others, thanks to a surrealist tone that flows through these pieces. If you have a want for exciting and left of field literature, I implore you to check this out."

— Thomas Moore, author of *Your Dreams, Forever, and Alone*

CONTENTS

CONTAINER

You will ease into the leather. Drive your slim frame into the car's black cushion. You treat it like a dream pillow. Your eyes blink in slow motion, when you look at me. A car passes. My fingers enjoy the firmness of the hand break, until you move them to your knee. You light a joint. I've said no smoking in the car before. You've never cared. Blow it in my face and laugh. Pass it to me. I edge the window down from the frame. Press of a button. Everything slows down. You shuffle your legs from side to side. Your feet are on the seat, on the dash. You say Let's go. I take a drink from the bottle.

The joint is in my mouth, smoke coiling around my face. The glimmering of the red light at which we are stopped cuts through the haze. A fog, a glowing red. A cop drives slowly across the light, doesn't look at us as he passes. The cop doesn't know that under your black pants are black fishnet stockings, but I know. You haven't told me, but I know. I've felt them, through the denim. I tell you, I could probably crush your skinny thigh if I squeezed hard enough. This makes you writhe. You take a firm pull. We exchange. I pass you the bottle. I try to move your hand down, so the cop won't see. You squirm away, into your little corner. Blowing more smoke in my face. You'd held it there, in your mouth. It rained last night. But it seems as if the road is still wet.

Our eyes first met in the elevator. I told myself I saw you in a dream. But I wouldn't have remembered that. I never remembered my dreams. I saw you more than I saw anyone else that lived there. We don't live there anymore. Little tilts of the head. Subtle smiles. Look at me, then downwards. At the broken tile. This elevator needs repairs. Maybe we'll get stuck in it, die in it. It took us 8 months to say anything.

You say to speed up. I warn you to have patience. Cops are everywhere tonight. The city feels violent. It wants to consume us, and everything in it. I know he's home, but I ask you if you're sure anyway, because it irks you. I ask, but you just give a look. A street lamp lights your face as we drive under it. My god you are beautiful. I can see you react when I say that. You're good at not giving much away, but in this moment your chest flattens, your back arches, your shoulders recede into the leather. Just a touch.

We've been banned from too many hotels. Too many people know my name.

I watered the plants for my neighbour. I hoped I'd run into you. You had that way of looking down, at an angle. And then back up at me. The elevator would grind upwards. Stuffed full. I'd see a sliver of your hair. One of your eyes pinned to mine. No one spoke. A muted cough broke the silence. I overheard you in the lobby. A friend in the building. I turned to look. I heard your voice.

You smiled at me. Stared at me with a knife in your hand. I imagined it would be easy enough to stab me. This box that must be discarded. You brought flowers down. The look of dried tears on your face. I didn't ask. We saw each other in the park. I can see your smile from far away. No more waiting. You got in. We smiled at each other. Every time. You asked me what was in the box. I said books and old photos. We made comfortable small talk. We were always good at that.

You told me that you were moving soon. Away from the apartment. Landlord was moving his daughter in. I felt a sinking feeling. You said it was for the better. Your husband would be much closer to his work. I suggested it would be good to exchange numbers and you agreed. We didn't text at all, until you left the building a month or two later. In the first text you sent me, you described how your ultimate desire was to be crushed in a collapsed elevator. I stared at the screen.

You reach into the glove box. My phone rings, and I see that it's my wife, and you swipe it before I can do anything. You stash the phone in the glove box and close it up. I press my foot into the pedal. We fly through the night. From city, to overpass, to open space. All darkly lit. Glowing, shooting past us like stars. The highway roars on. You grind yourself into the seat. Where should we go? Where is there left to go? Give me my phone. You reach into the glove box and pull out a small wrench that I'd forgotten was in there. You hold it up to your face and smile at me. My foot comes off the pedal. Velocity eases. You pout and shake your head, very slowly.

A gnawing sound in my guts. The tightening of elevator cables. A drowned noise.

A table cloth tied around a victim's face. I tell you I want you to destroy me.

You laugh and say you'll do anything. Anything for me. I want to abandon this life and everything in it. Breathe in only dust. Rays of sun that would melt my skin.

Turn to a crisped shell. I don't want to know your name. I cannot tolerate information. I want us to do bad things. I want to do bad things with you. You have a really nice smile but I can see behind it.

You stick your long tongue out. Dangle it, beside the metal. A drop of spit drips off. You don't know where that's been. The look on your face when I say that. You lap your tongue up the wrench, all the way, in slow motion. The hot white of the highway lights gleams off the metal. It shines in my face. You lick up and down, in super slow motion.

When we met that first night on the street, that first time outside the building, when you pushed me up against the neon backdrop, the lettered sign igniting the name of our city, your mouth pressed against mine for an endless segment in time, you said that I made you feel a rush, a feeling you hadn't felt in a while, a deep sensation way down, a feeling that you wanted to stab me. It made me grab you tighter.

Your one hand holds the wrench, while the other is down your pants. You lap at it like a dog. Spit falls to the floor of my car. On the black mats, by your feet. I imagine you on all fours, cleaning those filthy mats with your tongue. I know you would do it if I asked. You lick all inside the head of the wrench, like you're trying to find something with your tongue. You dangle your tongue out at me, laughing. You open the head of the wrench, stick your tongue in, and then tighten. You clamp the wrench on your tongue. I'm driving way too fast. If the cops clock me, we're done for. I may lose my license. Your tongue is now fully clamped in the ridges of the wrench. It is suspended in the air of the car. The wrench hangs off your mouth, spit dripping down, your smile as clear as the open highway.

You told me you wanted me to remove your flesh. I told you I'd like to go to work on your torso with a bat. You told me you'd cut off your tongue for me, place it in a jar. Solidify it in resin, place it on a podium adorned in gold and crystal. You told me you wanted to see me stung to death by giant hornets. I told you to suck the puss out of my wounds. You told me you wanted to be contained, crushed, by my body. I told you I'll gain so much weight, just to crush you with ease. You told me you'd like me to make you cry. I told you you won't have a voice. You told me you wished things were different. I told you they can be.

I don't know where we are going. I don't know where this highway ends. I don't know how far things can go. I don't know where you came from. I don't know where we fit in on this map. I don't know where the lights end, where the road will become lit only by our headlights. I don't know what time it is. I don't know when you need to be home. I don't know when your husband will start to worry, nor do I care. I don't know if you do either. I don't know if anything matters. If we are just particles, floating along. Or if we are more than that. I don't know if we'll see dead animals on the side of the road. I don't know if we'll enjoy it if we do. I won't know their story. I want to know these things. We can't know these things.

BIRD EATING GLASS

Mantle is asked who their preferred interviewer would be, between Katie O, Jackie B, and Lars V, and Mantle shrugs their skeletal shoulders so slowly, like mountains ascending during tectonic cataclysmic events, as if to leave this earth, only to return, to the frame, a breath of relief. Only a handful want the job. Their presence, Mantle's presence, is intimidating. But those who know them well say they are very nice.

In less than one year, Mantle has soared, from a months-long neck, neck, and neck Billboard race between Lil Grenade Launcher and Maya Kaya, to a lead of astronomical disparity that all other musicians who once thought themselves worthy of fame have now (probably) committed some form of ritual suicide.

Mantle once declared in an interview with Noisey's Gal Halpern that they have no influences, no clear sources of inspiration, and no history of engaging with any art form ever. Halpern told Mantle she did not believe them, laughing her uncomfortable way through the accusation. Mantle simply stared, black pupils unencumbered by the shuttering of eyelids, until she decided to move on to another question.

Mantle, in a green room, is handed a nail file, as some (but not all) of their fingernails are long to the point of improperness. Mantle holds the nail file up to the light, and then places it on a coffee table, next to three design books and two magazines about the music industry. There are also celebrity gossip magazines scattered about. It is a large, you could even say excessive, coffee table. Mantle's face is on some of those celebrity magazines. Mantle's unlikely face, twisted mouth, rotten jagged teeth, and all.

Sorg Sorgensen wrote a biography about Mantle that claimed all kinds of things. Mantle did not know about it at the time of publication. When asked about it, Mantle claimed they'd never heard of Sorg Sorgensen. When asked about the validity of the claims in the book, about Mantle's extreme upbringing, Mantle said that they did not know what the book claimed. When some details were described to the then 30-year-old (we think?) noise musician, now the best-selling musical recording artist of all time (a fact, regardless of what a biographer may or may not write), for example, the detail in the book of how when Mantle was six years old they were nearly killed by a particularly giant bald-eagle and suffered severe facial lacerations, hence the scars and the lower lip configured to permanently reveal a selection of jawline and teeth normally hidden on most people, and particularly ghastly looking in Mantle's case, Mantle denied the truth of that and all other anecdotes described in the book. Mantle was not in any way (at least visibly) bothered by these claims. But they were quick to deny any validity to them. Sorg Sorgensen had been labeled a fraud. Sorg Sorgensen was the fourth author to publish an unauthorized biography of Mantle. Mantle's lawyers encouraged them to sue. Mantle did not sue, or read any of these books.

Jackie B is chosen to interview Mantle for Scuzz magazine. Scuzz used to be considered niche. They are now staggeringly mainstream. But they have credibility. Because they interviewed Mantle before the big days. Among other things. Jackie B has never met Mantle. She is a newbie at Scuzz, but well-regarded as an interviewer, so she gets the gig. The interview is scheduled before Mantle's show at The Chain Reaction, in Anaheim, first day of the massive tour. Jackie B suggests to her editors that the interview should happen after the show. Her editors, namely Ronnie McGee, laugh off the suggestions. "Oh, you don't just interview Mantle after one of his shows." Jackie makes a mental note of McGee's misgendering of the six-foot-six amalgam of bone and greyish-white leather skin that is Mantle. "And why not?" she asks in a tone sharper than she would have liked, if she had better control.

"His shows take a lot out of him."

There have been several occasions where ambulances have been called to Mantle shows, mostly for a person or persons in the audience. Only seven people (eight if you count one who's been in a coma for three years) have died at Mantle shows.

Jackie B reads this information in the pamphlet that has been prepared for her by a Scuzz intern named Claye. Jackie B does not and could not know that Claye has Crohn's and wears a colostomy bag to work, as Claye had managed to keep this detail about herself secret from everyone other than her parents and her younger sister until recently, when she started to open up more about these things. She tells Jackie B this about herself as Jackie B reads her pamphlet. Claye tells Jackie B that listening to Mantle has changed her life, has encouraged her to open up more. Jackie B does not have Crohn's, but does have a tendency to develop severe bronchitis and has crippling anxiety about sex as a result of a traumatic assault when she was in high school. Jackie B and Claye both, separately, wonder about Mantle's past traumas. Maybe there are none of which to speak. But neither Jackie B nor Claye believe this to be likely.

Jackie B reads through archives of reviews and interviews with Mantle. She has yet to admit to any of her editors or publishers or other professional acquaintances that she has never listened to a single minute of Mantle's quote unquote music despite the fact that Mantle's quote unquote music is on extreme rotation at every radio station in the country, even the country stations. Jackie B has yet to admit that she has yet to listen to a single track of Mantle's music because she is scared. Scared she will be perceived as a fraud, fired, blacklisted. She has yet to listen to the music because she is scared of the music. She's heard it's a lot.

Mantle is unlike other musicians of their status in that Mantle only has one home. Most musicians of Mantle's status (there are none, at the moment. Mantle's status is higher than any other, at least in terms of sales or word-of-mouth popularity) have two homes. Or three. Or more. Mantle's home is in Los Angeles, and Mantle decides they will walk to the upcoming show, the night of.

Scuzz decides to go for the immersive and asks (suggests? encourages? mandates?) Jackie B to spend the day in Mantle's Lincoln Heights apartment before the actual interview. Jackie B says yes, and expresses some genuine excitement.

When she was little, around six but maybe seven, Jackie B had a stranger sneak up behind her and cut her blonde ponytail off with gardening shears. Charges were pressed. The perpetrator of the crime appeared to the naked eye to be, how might they put it, marginal? Marginalized? In terms of income and mental stability? He turned out to be the son of the owner of the Squickle Relish company, the heir to a relish fortune. Jackie B always wears her blonde hair in a tightly bound bun.

In Sorg Sorgensen's unauthorized biography, he

writes that Mantle is the son of a ballerina and metallurgist, both of whom died after becoming trapped in their panic bunker during a raging forest fire. There is no evidence to support this information anywhere in the known universe. It appears to be made up, but all things are made up by something, which is what Mantle said when asked about this biographical detail. No one takes Sorgensen's biography seriously, or any of the others, but people like to find and enjoy tidbits where they can; fragments, whisps, hints of the origins of things, even in the realm of the almost certainly fictional.

Jackie B surprises herself with how many hours of old interviews she watches to prepare, almost as if she can't stop, but she still does not listen to the music. She is stunned at the sound of Mantle's voice in these interviews, a voice which never makes it into the music. It isn't the kind of music that requires or benefits from vocals. Their voice is reminiscent of a whisper, but not an intentional whisper, more like the whisper of a throat once slashed by a whirring chainsaw blade that broke while severing the lifespan of a dying redwood, and managed to just barely keep their vocal cords viable, after months of intensive care and surgeries and rehab. It is the sound of furious struggle to make breath into words. Every word is a chore. Mantle sounds like someone that would rather not speak, not out of pretention, but self-preservation.

Scuzz informs Jackie B that the one-day stay in Mantle's Lincoln Heights, 1st floor, 770 sq ft apartment, a one-plus-den with one bath, with little in the way of natural light, in a building with peeling yellow walls and unknown liquid crystallizing along the outer stucco in a rust-stained rictus, a building where there have been murders, before and during Mantle's residency, will in fact be a three-day and two-night stay. Ronnie McGee and Scuzz feel it will add a sense of ominous authenticity to the whole exercise. They are marketing geniuses and always get things right. Jackie B is bright-eyed and not in a position to feel anything but super stoked about the prospect, at least not outwardly speaking. She wants to ask questions about things like sleeping arrangements. Her editor will have to call her back.

Jackie B watches tapes of an early show from many years back, when Mantle was still considered a cult phenomenon. She watches on mute, or her iPad. She is taken by this immense yet somehow diminutive frame of a person or being or whatever, operating keyboard and laptop, and a few devices unfamiliar to her, with such resounding intensity, that every press of key or button sends them into what can only be described as extreme rapturous shudders. The audience slowly comes to move in sequence with the grim carcass on stage. They are in throes.

Jackie B doesn't know this, but after that particular show, Mantle developed flesh-eating disease on their right leg and was hospitalized for two weeks and nearly had to say goodbye to the toxified limb. They now walk with a visible limp and will forever, or until death, or until they no longer walk, whichever comes first. Jackie B has never seen Mantle walk and does not know about the limp. But she will soon.

Jackie B has clear instructions; no time spent in the apartment is to be recorded or even remarked upon in any kind of public forum. This stay is to acclimatize her to this most significant of artists, to put her in the right zone to conduct the interview, and nothing more. Authenticity. Jackie B tries not to worry...

She regrets not bringing a scarf. She laments the last hug of afternoon sun before Mantle welcomes her in, covered in their customary oversized black robes, squinting like a creature of the dark unable to tolerate sun, hiding their face until the bubbly-looking interview girl is inside, past the dim front foyer with the flickering halogens, into the gloom of the apartment. Jackie B feels, immediately upon stepping foot into the apartment, that she really should have brought at least a scarf and maybe a jacket and maybe ear muffs. She can see her breath.

Mantle does not make offers. They escort her into the main room where there is no furniture. There is a keyboard on the ground and several amps and a laptop and some pedals and other music-adjacent type machines of which Jackie B couldn't name if it were Final Jeopardy and Alex Trebek was still alive and well and pointing a loaded pistol at her abdomen. Mantle sits on the ground and does things on the computer. Jackie B shivers. Mantle doesn't wait long before removing their black robe, a move that at first startles Jackie B, who doesn't want to consider what might be happening, something like sexual harassment, or worse, but they hand her the robe without incident. It takes her a minute to take it, and longer to adjust into it. She wrestles with the giant caves of fabric, taking five full minutes to pull her head through. It is heavy and warm and she can still see her breath but less so. Maybe that's just her imagination. Maybe it all is, imagination. The room is dark and grey and musky and blue, and the slivers of afternoon sun can't brighten it.

Jackie B finds herself staring at Mantle's naked body, naked except for tiny white underwear. Their ribs and uneven spinal bones are plainly visible, surrounding skin lined with scars that she thinks maybe could have come from the lash of a box jellyfish, because she remembers during her years obsessed with venomous aquatic creatures of Australia that she took particular interest in the beauty of the stinging pattern of the box jellyfish, one of Australia's deadliest animals. She asks if the scars are from a box jellyfish, her first words to Mantle since entering the apartment, first words since "Hi, I'm Jackie B!" which she said on the stoop, but Mantle has noise canceling headphones in and doesn't hear her. She also notes the pallor of their skin, grey, like the room itself, not pale exactly, but that's probably what most people would call it. So pale it can't quite be human, can it? She never, during the whole stay, or for a time after, feels she can describe Mantle's face. Not because Mantle doesn't have a face (they do), but because she is too afraid to look straight at it.

When Jackie B eventually uncrosses her cramping legs and goes to the bathroom (and unknowingly gets a small dribble of pee on the black robe. She will never know this occurred and as significant events in the universe are ranked by importance, this places low), she is afforded the opportunity on her way back to look into the small den, which appears to have been converted into a recording studio. There's minimal equipment, foam-insulated walls, and a staggering collection of metal objects, bricks, hammers, trash, poles, rust, leather, discarded things found in alleys and trash bins, in dumpsters, in L.A.'s abandoned corners. Much noise is made in here, she gathers. Much noise she cannot hear.

Sorg Sorensen wrote that one of Mantle's famous tracks, one of the most difficult to listen to, one of the most critically acclaimed, was recorded in Antarctica, on the windiest, stormiest day of the decade on the frozen continent.

Jackie B had intended to suggest she and Mantle go for dinner in Koreatown, to a place she loves where they serve an eclectic mix of modern Korean, Japanese, and Peruvian food, but since entering the space which Mantle inhabits, she now understands this to be an unavailable suggestion. She won't bother. She orders Thai food through UberEATS, which she can easily expense. She orders more than enough for both of them, and makes it clear to Mantle that they should feel free to partake, but Mantle declines to eat anything. She eats while standing as they continue to do things with sounds on a computer that only they can hear.

Jackie B noted moments in the tapes, in past interviews, moments which felt to her like something profound or significant was being reflected upon. Like the time Kip Cars asked Mantle if they were religious, to which Mantle said, "If I am religious, I hope I am going to hell. But I don't think I am, so unfortunately I must stay here for the time being." In an interview with Gillian Killian of Wired, when asked about where inspiration comes from, Mantle simply said, "I have no choice." When asked to elaborate, they shrugged, and then became visibly frightened, as if being watched by some entity from beyond this plane. When asked by Joyce O'Keeffe of Bon Appetit what Mantle liked to eat, they said, "I am nourished by sound alone." When O'Keeffe claimed she didn't buy that, Mantle said, "Most food would be wasted on me, would do serious damage to me, on the inside. Like a bird eating glass." O'Keeffe spent the remainder of the interview wondering why they, a food publication, had booked time with this person. It was on her mind and all over her face, you could tell. She remarked on that interview, later, in her own interview with Oprah, saying, "Fame is a slut."

Jackie B is offered Mantle's bed, a plain single mattress on the bedroom floor. She declines. Mantle doesn't exactly insist, but reminds Jackie B they do not have an alternative, only bare floor. Jackie B smiles and says "I've slept on worse!" and goes to bed at 9 P.M. with a white towel over her robed body as an extra blanket.

By midnight, still unable to sleep, she sheepishly nudges Mantle and, with some shame and embarrassment, asks if the offer is still available. Mantle doesn't hesitate; they take up Jackie's space on the floor, and Jackie molds herself into the contours of the mattress. It is more comfortable than she expected. She breathes into herself.

In the morning, Jackie B is startled awake by cacophonous, miserable hammering; crashing, twisting, gnawing metal sounds. Glass breaking. Unpleasantness all around. The sound studio may be insulated but it has no door, it's just a little den after all. It's still mostly dark out. She sees her breath in the bleak dawn light. She is reminded of camping as a child in Yellowstone when a grizzly waded in rain puddles outside their tent, in the early spring morning. The grizzly stuck its nose through the tent door, which had been left open by her urinating father, who was nowhere to be seen, its brown-soaked fur stinking, dripping, emanating steam. She saw the grizzly's breath, in utter silence, frozen solid, as she sees it now. Ungodly loudness that she should cover her ears to protect against violates her sense of reason, but she does not cover them. She does not protect. She listens. The noise shouldn't be bearable, but somehow it is.

There is no coffee maker, but she chooses not to leave. She goes uncaffeinated for the first time in three years, when she had the flu and saw her dead grandmother sitting on her legs, scrubbing at her ghostly eyeballs with sandpaper, during the height of her fever.

Midway through the day, Mantle hands Jackie headphones. It is time for her to hear. Her eyes go wide as Mantle plugs them into the computer and presses the spacebar.

Birds fly off the trees outside the little window, in unison. They won't come back anytime soon.

The room is steeped in grey. She listens. The headphones cancel outer sound. Mantle can't hear it, but of course knows what she is hearing.

In an interview with Jamila Homes of Pitchfork, Mantle was asked when exactly they came out as non-binary, and what made them make that decision at the time. Mantle made a face with a furrowed brow. They rubbed their bald head, a head that looked as if it had never housed one follicle of hair. Mantle's face bore the struggle of confusion. They did not understand the question.

Jackie B listens to Mantle's entire discography without pause, sixteen hours of straight noise, some of it impossibly famous, some of it b-sided and under all radars, unavailable to anyone but her in this moment. Jackie B does not think to eat or dream. She moves only twice, both times to use the bathroom, both times bringing the computer and headphones with her.

It's late and black, middle of the dark morning, when both Mantle and Jackie B retire for sleep. Mantle sleeps in the corner, and Jackie B takes her own corner, not on the mattress, not covered by a blanket. Mantle tells her to take the bed. She refuses. She says, "It's your bed."

The third day, Mantle doesn't work. They sit, maybe meditative, unclear to Jackie B how deliberate this state is. She is very hungry and decides to leave the apartment to get cereal and milk from the Arco gas station four minutes down the road. The sun burns her eyes and lights her face. The warmth is unwelcome. People stare. She wants Honey Nut Cheerios but they don't have Honey Nut Cheerios, only the knockoff Sweetened-O's, which she settles for. The clerk's nametag says Maurice and he has a half-grey, half-black pencil-thin goatee and is standoffish, which Jackie B realizes is not out of disdain or ire, but out of fear. She can smell it. Only on her walk back does she register that she is still wearing Mantle's heavy black robe. She sniffs her armpits.

Back inside she sees her breath again. Mantle lies on the floor. Is it meditation or prayer?

Jackie B gets a call. The show, which is in two days, has been moved from The Chain Reaction to The Staples Center, which means ten times as many tickets are being issued. They have already gone on sale and they have already sold out. This stunt was always going to go this way. She should have known. The interview will be conducted after the show. She gets her wish. Scheduling sometimes does win out. She is told to dress nice. They will be going out after.

She doesn't remember going home. Things have gelled into a blur, and the present is gone.

Jackie B, home for one day before the show, which will kick off a worldwide tour, sits staring off into space until it's time for sleep, during which she has horrible nightmares. She wakes up in the night and downloads all of Mantle's available music and listens in the dark. It helps with the aftershock of the nightmares. She eventually sleeps without fear.

Mantle's very first live performance was in front of sixteen people at a venue called Wheelbound, in a bike-shop basement in Boise, Idaho, which is not where Mantle is from, but was the first venue that agreed to host them, in which they performed with one small keyboard in the middle of a child-sized half-pipe. Three people in the audience vomited and one had a seizure. Another, a seventeen-year-old girl with a red buzzcut and red mascara, fell down the stairs later in the evening, during the headliner, and suffered a compound break of the femur. After her red-streaked tears ran semi-dry, she lit a lighter while being taken away in the ambulance, and held it up, swaying, as the morphine took hold.

Jackie B takes a limo to the Staples Center with Ronnie McGee and an assortment of other colleagues, because Scuzz magazine knows how to arrive in style. McGee wears sunglasses and has his hair in a ponytail, which Jackie B stares at, while imagining garden shears. She drinks champagne in a private box from high up, with coworkers, record execs, media people, some athletes, stars. Taylor Swift is there. The show takes an unreasonable amount of time to start and there is no opening act. When the lights start to dim, Jackie's urge not to be around these people grows until she can't bear it, and she abandons her flute on the ledge of a Ficus planter, ignoring Ronnie McGee's confused cries after her as she leaves the box, takes the stairs, past the flood of fans still in the tangential tunnels of the arena, and uses her press pass to allow security to grant her access to the floor, where she squishes between perspiring sacks of flesh and black cloth, smoke, ecstasy, chains, boots, smells of many kinds, both recklessly dirty and overly clean, as an ambient hum that sounds like gale winds fills the auditorium. This sound has been encroaching for some time. It is only detectable now, but she knows it's always been there. She elbows her way as close to the stage as she can, and cranes her neck.

Sorg Sorgenson, at the present moment, is not at the show. He is in his home city of Copenhagen, dining at Noma, where he is served a dish containing the rare Helsing berry, to which neither he nor the restaurant staff know he is severely allergic. Sorg Sorgensen breathes in the aroma of the wondrous dish. The smell alone is magic. He is transported. He takes his first bite as, 5608 miles west, Mantle takes the stage.

Mantle wears a white dress. It is not necessarily a wedding dress, in that it does not bear the look of a dress that would be interpreted as having the primary use of ornamenting a bride, but it does appear to be a dress that could be worn by a bride of modern tastes, should that bride choose to deviate from what someone might call convention. The stage is set, keyboard and laptop and wall of amps. Any audience member not wearing earplugs is about to suffer. Jackie B does not wear earplugs. The thought hadn't occurred to her. Mantle bows, and strikes the first key, and their body responds to the pulverizing weight of the decibel level, of the thing called noise music but the thing that is so much more than that, erupting out of the towers of speakers, out of the crust of the earth. Mantle reacts to the sounds of their creation with violent tremors, as does much of the audience.

Mantle is asked regularly in interviews if their wiry frame is ever hurt from the constant involuntary thrashing their live music elicits. "Always," they say.

During the 97 minutes that Mantle is on stage, no visible injury from an outside source befalls them. But, the dress, once white, begins to turn red in spots. Most observer-listeners are too enraptured to notice or care or understand. Jackie B notices. As Mantle aches through the performance, the blood soaks through, until the entire garment is dark red. Jackie B imagines blood leaking from Mantle's ripped-open scars, from their skin peeled apart by the very force of the music, from every pore of their body, from deep within.

Mantle's blood soaks the dress so thoroughly it no longer appears red at all. It has become black. The weight of it begins to cause rips in the fabric. The dripping black garment, similar enough to Mantle's day-to-day robe, becomes tatters over the passing of time. Jackie B, essentially deaf, in a moment of terrified all-consuming clarity, wonders how she will conduct an interview in this state, hers or theirs. The volume is an annihilating weight, a compactor, closing in, crushing her eardrums to dust. She beats her head, hoping for a sound. Soon, all is auditory hollow wind, even as Mantle thrashes on stage, thrashes more violently than ever before. Some audience members fall on top of each other. Some scream. All are ecstatic.

When she was a teenager, a boy Jackie B liked, Bryan Santos, got hit by a car while skateboarding across a busy intersection, skateboarding across the intersection to her, to meet her. She remembered the sound of the metal trucks of the skateboard colliding with the steel of the hood, the cracking of glass. The sounds of crunching, breaking, of things not supposed to happen. She rushed into the intersection, to meet her young love, who lay dazed, bleeding from the head and arm. She held his hand, waiting for the ambulance, unable to hear anything but the echoes of collision, and eventually sirens. She rushes the stage but can't because the crush of bodies is too thick, so she taps a shoulder much taller than her, and points up, and though it's not really that kind of show, and the cocktail dress she foolishly wears will become ripped to scraps, she is thrust atop the sea of the crowd, on shoulders and heads, feeling as if on a wave, as Mantle kneels, pouring sweat, barely able to hang on, fingertips on the white and black keys, and Jackie B is thrown in directions she can't control, and she sees in her mind the glorious union for which she hopes and needs, because the person on stage needs it, needs her, needs help, medical or spiritual or otherwise. She is thrust. Fingers fall off the keys. She believes, maybe, she can make out the crowd's roar. She reaches out, to try to touch Mantle, but she's too far away. Mantle lies face down on the stage, and the crowd screams with catharsis and jubilation, and Mantle, from the ground, face down, reaches out too, which Jackie B believes, knows, is for her. She reaches, but she cannot reach.

Does Anyone Care How the Vegetable Oil Feels?

I knew this fucking writer who every time he wanted to write something he'd go way deep in the zone and live the shit hard. I asked him do you call it method writing or some shit and he chased me with a butcher knife. One time he wanted to write a story about a drummer who was manic depressive and a maniac genius and this was definitely way before that fucking Whiplash movie came out except he didn't know shit about drums or music, the writer I mean, he just liked jazz and death metal. He bought a drum kit off this retired drummer dude who used to play in twenty different bands and was 6 foot 4 and 400 pounds. He pounded this kit all night not knowing what the ever-loving fuck he was doing, and the old lady that lived downstairs came up three times, and she was hard of hearing as shit. His hands didn't bleed like in that movie, but I think out of frustration he took a knife and cut his palms open and as he was spewing blood all over his floor he decided the drummer in the story would have to be a total lunatic who howled at the moon so he went out and howled for hours and wrapped his hands in J-cloths and we got really drunk, vomiting and everything, then later he got nerve damage.

He was obsessed with porcupines and wanted to write a story about one named Barbara, so he went out into the country and trapped one, don't ask me how. He came back with it thrashing around in a net, his hands and chest already stuck with quills. He said his dad called him porcupine. This thing lived in his apartment for weeks, rampaging around all pissed off but eventually it chilled out and then later it died and he was so sad, even though he'd no longer be impaled with quills. I meant to ask him why his dad called him porcupine but I forgot and then it was too late.

I brought Emma over once, I'd just told her he was a writer I looked up to, and not much else and she seemed to like that I was spending time with other writers, people from whom I could learn, but when we got there and she said so you're a writer huh he said no I'm an accountant and she said oh, I thought you were a writer and he said no I'm an accountant. She nodded and looked confused and looked at me and he said writers are fags and I wasn't about to begin trying to explain him to her, who knew what the fuck he was working on at the time. Then later a guy he was dating came over and they made out a bit and Emma was more confused.

I just wanted to spend more and more time around him and Emma did ask about that, but I just enjoyed being in the room with the guy, like everyone else did. Magnetic shit. After he died I felt numb and like shit and thought about trapping porcupines but didn't. I didn't tell her that he died, I still haven't told her. She probably doesn't know, why would she.

The last thing I remember him working on was a story told from the perspective of a bottle of vegetable oil that had been on the same grocery store shelf for nine years. He said he'd been writing the fucking thing for nine years and had erased and chopped and rewritten more than he could remember, and still only had 325 words. He was obsessed with this fucking batshit story. He couldn't type anymore because of the nerve damage in his hands so he recorded the story on a voice recorder but his voice was shot from smoking glass so he had me come over a few times to help him record the thing, but I'd say a few sentences the way he told me to then he'd shake and go nuts and scream no no no it's all fucking wrong! His apartment was littered with empty bottles of canola oil, I'm talking hundreds. He had one full bottle on the kitchen counter, looking down at us while we worked. I asked him about that story later, and in his broken voice he said ah fuck that stupid shit, I'm done with it, but I knew he was lying. I just knew. He was thinking about that story all the time, right then and there, as we spoke. I just knew.

For Whom I Bare My Teeth

They'd lived there two days and the place was already trashed. Rick secured the sublet through a friend of a friend; neither of their names were on the lease. It was a small, first-floor one-bedroom, with a cramped, moldy basement that could store old boxes and not much else. Ultimate luxury compared to their last place, but three times the commute for Sarah to Marden's, where she worked the perfume counter. After the first week, the hardwood floor was covered in empty beer cans, gin bottles, Bordeaux corks, burger wrappers, cigarette butts. Sarah made Rick smoke outside, which lasted a full 12 hours, until he said fuck that, and she couldn't stop him.

In the second week she came home to a dead porcupine on the floor with a plastic trash bin on its head. Rick lay soaking in the bathtub, yanking quills out of his leg in the bloody water. He said he brought the animal home for his writing. Not for research, but for something to do with authenticity. He said "We got up to some crazy shit, me and Gerald. He couldn't handle it, now he's gone." Sarah counted in her head the previous dead animals she'd found. This was the second one he'd named Gerald.

She'd cleaned up his blood before, more than once. The first time was in the early days, when they took MDMA and planned for a long fun night, but Rick tripped taking off his pants and brained himself on the fireplace mantle. He'd also popped Viagra but didn't tell her. They sat in the ER with a blanket over his lap, ice and bloody towel on his head. The hospital was packed, sirens sounding in the hot night outside, and patients kept flooding in. Five men rushed forward, one of them holding his arm, the others narrating the knife fight to the triage nurse in a drugged frenzy, talking over each other like screaming birds. Sarah watched the cascade of blood, from arm to floor, pooling around white sneakers. She stared at it, high and delirious, licking her lips, jerking her unconscious boyfriend off under the blanket, the blood pooling.

After the first week she got sick of the city bus, the constant smoke wafting in her face, the smell of shit, the non-existent schedule, the half-drunk drivers, so she took Ubers to work every day after that. She had a few regulars at the perfume counter. They'd come in once or twice a week to get good stuff for their wives and really good stuff for their mistresses. She buttered them up, beady-eyed, rose lipstick gleaming, making them splurge on the fancy stuff. Her boss, Danielle, when she wasn't blitzed on Percocet or lithium, made mental notes to give Sarah a raise for being the best salesperson. Mental notes. Sarah had fair skin and light hair and wore all black, black leggings and a black blazer and a black shirt that revealed just enough. After work she'd take the Uber not quite home, have it drop her off five blocks away, in front of Sven's Liquor and Cleaning Supply, where she'd buy a bottle of red wine or a bottle of gin or both, and sometimes Veuve Clicquot.

"Why do *we* have to blow money on fancy shit? Bubbles," Rick said, "are all the same trash. Just get the seven-dollar prosecco."

"Why do we have to blow money? Whose money? *My* money? Are you kidding?"

"Hey. We're a unit. It's our money."

Rick was working on a new novel that he claimed had over 1000 characters, all of whom were addicted to drugs or crazy or both, and he needed to get intimately acquainted with each and every one of them. He said the porcupine thing was for one of the characters, a meth addict named Hans that believed he was a porcupine. Rick had been working on novels his whole life. He came close to finishing one of them, but said it just didn't feel right when he got near the end. This one, he said, was the real deal.

Sarah cooked light dinners and they ate at the breakfast bar on two barstools which Rick stole from the Irish pub down the block, when he and the scraggly albino bartender got drunk after last call. Rick waited him out, and once he passed out, face down in a puddle of warm stout, Rick made off with two stools. After dinner he and Sarah would drink another bottle of wine or maybe gin, and watch whatever was on TV. Sometimes they fell asleep on the couch. They didn't usually eat much.

One night during their second week in the place Sarah fell asleep on the couch after dinner, and Rick, on a dose of ketamine, took a shovel and broke apart a circle in the middle of the living room, a foot in diameter. He brought the shovel down like a spike, splintering the wood, until he'd made a pit. He brought in rocks from outside, talking to himself about the fires of hell and the purple toes of god, dumping rocks in the new hole. He threw the splintered wood on top, the new kindling. Sarah woke to crackling, the smell of smoke. Rick sat in front of the fire, rocking back and forth, naked.

"I'm going to bed," she said, seizing an open bottle of wine by the neck.

*

"Why don't you ever smile in pictures?" Rick asked, looking at an old photo of Sarah with her high school friends. All teeth bared except for hers. All hair blonde except for hers.

"Literally how many times must we go over this?"

"Like, since before I knew you, you've never shown those pearly perfect whites. Come on, let the world see 'em."

Sarah sipped Veuve Clicquot from a wine glass, and orange juice separately from a coffee mug. It was nine in the morning on a Saturday, their first full month in the place. The fire pit had embers still going. All walls on the main floor were smoked black.

Rick lit a cigarette.

"I really wish you wouldn't smoke near the Veuve."

"I read your phone last night, after you passed out," he said.

She pretended to ignore him, but he sat staring at her. She put her glass down.

"No, you didn't. You don't know my password."

"So, who is Oliver?" He said the name as if they both knew it was a fake name.

"Are you fucking serious? You piece of shit! How did you get in my phone?"

"After all I do for us."

"Calm down, he's a client from work." She took a large gulp.

"'How about you come for a ride sometime soon, I'll take you to the best restaurants in the city. We could even go to Paris.' Really sounds like a sale."

"You know I have to get cute with these dweebs. That's the job! Nothing has ever happened. Have you seen this guy? Please."

"Of course I haven't seen him. I did see his text where he said all those nice things about your 'perfect, tiny body.'"

"He's almost sixty, and he looks like an overcooked chicken thigh with a goatee."

Rick looked at her.

"I'm sorry I went through your phone."

Sarah nodded. "He does drive a big Mercedes," she said.

"What the fuck! Which one??"

"How should I know?"

"The E series?"

"Oh my god, don't ASK me about car types! You

know how crazy that makes me."

"Is it the fucking E series, like the long sleek one, or is it an SL? Like a two-door racer type?"

"Neither. It's an SUV. The black boxy one, like the Germans used in the war."

"Oh great! A fucking Nazi is trying to fuck my girlfriend!"

"You'd probably like that wouldn't you? I bet you picture it all the time."

"My grandfather is spinning in his grave!"

"I'm going to be late for work!" she said, swiping her phone off the counter, spilling the last few drops of champagne. The glass fell and broke as she walked away.

Rick cleaned it up, slicing his finger. He threw all the glass in the sink. Drops of blood mixed with the water on the counter. He grabbed the first rag he could find and scrubbed it up quickly. The blood kept flowing. He scrubbed quickly as he could, looking toward the bedroom.

*

Sarah came home from work to find Rick sitting around the fire pit with three skinny blonde shirtless men. They seemed like adults, but projected prepubescence. Village of the Damned on Adderall. They were tall, even while sitting she could tell. The fire was mostly embers. They davened in front of it, like it was the holy spirit.

"Rick," Sarah hissed. No one moved. She prodded him with her selfie stick. He didn't move, so she clubbed his bare back with the thing. It made the sound of a mallet slapping meat. He groaned, looked around.

"Yes, dear?" He yawned.

"Who are they?" she whispered.

The three blondes left the trance together, turned to Sarah. All waved.

"Sandro, Phell, Turner, say hi to Sarah."

"Hi," the middle one said. Phell.

"You're very small. Tiny, even. A little molecule," the tallest of three said. His voice was soft, girlish.

"Little molecule," Sandro said. "LM. We can call you that."

"Hmmm, yeah, hi, no thank you," she said. She sighed, heavy. Rick played with Sandro's hair, and she sighed louder, to no avail. She took the small Bordeaux bottle out of her paper bag. Sven's didn't have the normal kind she liked so she was forced to get a half bottle. There were no clean glasses in the cupboard. The sink was overflowing. A quick glance in and she saw broken glass crushed under old dishes. She used the rusty corkscrew and popped the moldy cork halfway until it got stuck, and used her teeth to drag it clear, splashing her chin with wine. She spit the cork out, scooped up the drips of wine with her hand, keeping it from her clothes, licking her fingers. She licked what she could from her chin, and sat around the fire, drinking straight from the bottle.

Phell produced a glass pipe and loaded a chalky white chunk into the chamber. The fire pit crackled. Embers hit the floor. No one moved to put them out. Phell lit the pipe, and thick, chrome-colored smoke blew into Sarah's face. She choked, had to duck out of the way. Her eyes watered. Turner muttered, speaking at the fire. Sarah watched Rick watch Turner's lips like a man possessed. She reached into her pocket and produced the tiny Louis Vuitton clutch. She admired it like a jewel in the sun.

Phell handed her the pipe. She took it without thinking.

"Try some," he said. She looked him in the eyes.

"I'm good, thanks."

Rick sat up, his arms propping him up from the ground.

"Come on," he said. "It's fun." Phell handed her the lighter.

Sarah rolled her eyes, flicked the lighter four times until the flame came, and ignited the rock. She sucked the smoke back until her lungs screamed, coughing it all out, trying to find her breath. She coughed like never before. Rick rubbed her back.

She clutched the thing for her life. Rick watched her stare at the fire. Her eyes were black. She revealed the slightest bit of tooth. Rick watched, while the three brothers stared and rocked back and forth at the fire. Sandro held a knife, ran it against his forearm. A line of blood flowed out, down his arm. Turner took the arm, held it in his lap, watching the blood. Sarah, black eyes fixed on the LV clutch, smelled the air. Her eyes took aim at the arm. Her one sharp exposed tooth dug into her lip.

"What is that?" Rick said.

Sarah, like the blonde brothers, stared at the bloody arm. Her black pupils twitched, her nails digging into the clutch. Her pink nail polish began to chip.

"It's the glowing stream of life," Phell said.

Sarah's tooth drove the skin of her pink lip into a

crater, tight like a balloon. Her eyes were rigid.

"What is that?" Rick said, trying to grab the clutch out of her hands. "Is this shit real? You spent two months' rent on this stupid thing? What the fuck."

She stared at the arm. Her tooth pierced her lip. Blood dribbled down her mouth.

"Like for real? Champagne, fucking fancy wine. Now this? Bullshit! We're gonna be out on our ass!"

She licked her lip. She ran her finger along it, smearing her ring in blood, and licked the ring.

"I didn't buy it," she said.

"Look how small it is. Can't stash much in there other than drugs. Maybe it's not so bad. We can share it."

"It was a gift."

"From who?"

"Guess."

"Don't do this to me."

"Guess."

"What's his name. I can't remember. The regular. Mercedes Nazi fucking guy."

"Oliver."

"Yeah, that."

"Yeah. That. Correct."

Rick shot up and scooted out of sight, to the bathroom, slamming the door. The brothers didn't notice or care. They all stared at Sandro's bleeding forearm. Sarah stared, smiling, flames dancing in her huge black eyes.

*

The three brothers got Rick a job as the night host

at a karaoke bar that their father owned. Rick worked Wednesday to Sunday, from six in the evening until three in the morning, while Sarah did Monday to Friday at Marden's, regular day shift hours. Rick didn't want the job, but they couldn't cut it on Sarah's income alone anymore. He had told her for months that he would sell his new book for a six-figure deal, but he had barely started writing it. He accepted his fate and took the job. He figured he'd have plenty of time to write in his notebook during the downtime. How busy could the place be? He spent every night managing drunken brawls, trying to talk security out of quitting, cleaning up pee and spilled beer and whatever else off the floor. All tasks he had no stomach for. He was miserable from the start. After several numb weeks of too much work, erratic sleep, and not enough drugs, he still hadn't been paid.

On the Friday of his fourth week he walked out, after the security guard Cedar, a former cop who got canned for selling pills on the job, called him a know-nothing dipshit. He pissed in Cedar's gas tank before hopping on the bus home.

When Rick got to the apartment, he saw the black Mercedes truck in the driveway. He stood frozen, staring at the license plate that read OWNR, while the crickets chirped and the wind made the trees sway like drunken giants. He looked around.

He unlocked the front door, let himself in while trying not to make a sound. The house was silent, except for the crackling embers in the firepit. The Louis Vuitton clutch sat on the entranceway table. He grabbed it, seething, and tossed it into the firepit. Thick, greenish smoke spewed around it for a while, until it burst into flames. It had something in it, maybe lipstick, or other makeup. Felt heavy for its size. He didn't care. He looked at the shoes near the front. Sarah's were there, as were a pair of black men's dress shoes.

He put his hand on the bedroom doorknob, put his ear to the wood. There was no sound. He opened the door, saw the room was empty. The bathroom was empty too. He looked around, trying to make sense out of it.

He put his ear to the basement door. He could just barely hear it, but there was a sound coming from down there. Could have been nothing, pipes, a rat. He opened the door, heard the sound more clearly. A wet sound. He left the light off, but was surprised no one jumped or gasped. They had to know he was there.

He started down the stairs but slipped in something, and tumbled down. Sarah didn't shriek even as he landed nearly on top of her, on both of them. Rick tried to stand but couldn't right his hands. They kept slipping on the wet ground.

"What the fuck?"

Sarah didn't acknowledge him. The sound continued.

He found the light switch. First all he saw was blood. On the ground. On his own clothes and hands. Sarah was at the body, at the leg, like a hyena. Rick tried to look around her, at the limb, which was mostly gone. Gnawed flesh. He saw white bone, poking through chewed red pulp. The whole leg was gone. Thread of torn black fabric ripped away. Pieces of the fabric floated in blood. Sarah continued feeding.

"Jesus fucking Christ, not again," Rick said. Sarah

didn't react. She continued to chew at Oliver's body.

"Sarah!" Rick screamed, grabbing her shoulder. She spun around, and he jumped back. She sat in a squat, her eyes glowing balls. Her entire face was drenched in blood. Not a spot of clear skin. Her black blazer, all her clothes, were soaked. She looked up at him. It was an innocent look, but he didn't get close.

"Sarah. What the fuck."

"What?" she said. "He said he wanted to come over." She bared her jagged teeth as she giggled. Rick got a good look at the fangs that even he rarely saw. Blood dripped off her jaw.

"What if I had people with me? Phell, Turner?"

Sarah shrugged. "More the merrier."

"This isn't funny. You said this wouldn't happen again."

Sarah stood up. She was a foot shorter than Rick, but he backed away from her. She grabbed his hand to her breast, and with her other hand grabbed his crotch. She kissed him, pulling his neck down to her, smearing blood on his face.

"We need to figure this out, pronto. The fucking guy's car is in our driveway."

She grabbed hold of Rick's neck and threw him down, into the puddle. She stood above him, stepping on his chest.

"Sarah, come on, now's really not the time –"

"Shh," she said. She squatted onto her lover's frame. Her eyes glowed. Her hair appeared to have grown longer. Even under her tiny frame, Rick could feel the immense strength of what was on top of him. She massaged his cock, her other hand on his throat. Blood dripped down from her mouth.

"Shut up," she said.

*

Sarah sat at the breakfast bar in her bathrobe, legs resting on the counter. She picked bits of flesh out of her teeth with a nail file.

Rick worked the phone. His hands were shaking.

"Hello, yes. Um, yes I'm calling because I need to replace a key fob for my car. I accidentally left it in Memphis, at my sister's, and apparently her Bichon Frise swallowed the thing, thinking it was one of his toys. I know, stupid dog right? Oh, it's a G Class, the 400 D. My name? Can't I just come in and pick one up? Do you really need the info? I see. Well, it's not for me, it's actually for my brother. It's his car, and I don't know if he's using his current name or his pen name. He's a relatively well-known playwright but he does in fact use a pseudonym. Who? Oh, I suppose I can pay for it. How much is the new fob? 800 fucking dollars? Are you kidding me?"

Rick hung up. Sarah looked at him, eyes wide.

"Sounds expensive," she said.

"Yeah, it is."

"Just like my clutch was, you inconsiderate asshole."

"Why in fuck did you put the guy's car keys inside your purse!"

"It's not a purse, it's a custom-made Louis Vuitton clutch! He had it made for me! And I had his keys in it because he said I could drive the car later! He wanted me to hang onto the keys, to get me excited! And you know what, I was excited to drive it!"

"Listen. We have to figure out how to move this fucking guy's car. This guy's obviously got money, people must know him around here. They will come looking for him. It's fucking sitting in our driveway."

"You should have thought about that before you decided to torch my beautiful gift."

She picked a little grey sliver of muscle out of her tooth, examined it on the end of the nail file, and flung it at Rick.

"Jesus, ew!"

"Grow up."

"Sarah, this is serious. We've gotta get rid of that car. Or we've got to ditch this place."

"You know what? I think you should call the Hanson triplets."

"What? Why? Are you nuts?"

"Invite them over. I'm in the mood to see more people."

"What do you mean?"

"Don't worry about what I mean. Just call them. Have them come over."

"Come on. Stop. We've got to clean up down there."

"Call them. We can have a party. The five of us." Rick noticed Sarah playing with herself, through her robe. Some dried blood remained on her cheek. She was licking at it.

Rick looked up to the ceiling.

"I'm hungry," she said.

"God damn it."

She stood up. Rick jumped up, backing away from the fire pit.

"I'm going out," she said.

"Where?"

"To eat."

She marched out the door in her bathrobe.

*

The sun was blinding. It was brighter than she ever remembered. She walked, delirious. She felt she had been walking for miles. She didn't notice that there was some blood on the white bathrobe, but she wouldn't have cared. She couldn't stop tonguing at her teeth.

She looked around, for a neighbour. She spotted a man and woman with a stroller. She could see the baby's arms jutting out, hands clutching at air.

"Sarah!" she heard Rick behind her, coming out of the house. She continued down the street, saw the bus coming. She ran to the bus stop, letting the wind blow the robe wide open. The man walking the stroller turned and stared, and his wife smacked him.

The bus door opened and Sarah got on. The bus driver stared at her. He'd seen her many times before, but not like this. Rick got on behind her as the doors closed. The other passengers stared. Sarah ran her hands up the bus driver's arm.

"Miss?"

"I never realized you were so strong," she said.

Rick grabbed her arm and dragged her to the back of the bus.

"Hey! The fares!"

"I'll come back and pay in a second, just go!" Rick said. He sat her down at the back corner and wedged himself in beside her.

"What are you doing?" he whispered. "You've got to chill. Deep breaths. Just let this pass."

"You are being a major buzzkill right now," she said.

"You're flashing a bus full of people in a bloodstained robe," he said. "We're gonna get fucking arrested."

"Who asked you to tag along!"

"Shh!"

"What about her?" Sarah said, pointing at a girl sitting a few seats up. She couldn't have been older than 15.

"What about her?"

"I want to go say hi to her."

"Just sit here and relax." He held her wrists tight.

"You know if I wanted to, I could break both your hands," she said. She broke free and grabbed Rick's crotch.

"Let's just get you some food. Like normal food," Rick said.

"We'll stop at the mall. We could bring a guy into the bathroom. For old-time's sake. You could watch me bite it off and swallow it whole."

Rick could feel the sweat dripping down his back. Sarah's grip tightened. She started licking his neck.

"Please be careful," he said.

"Always," she said. "With you. My love."

"Just, careful."

The bus stopped, and Sarah leapt out of the seat. She was off the bus faster than Rick could fathom. She knew he'd follow behind. She raced through the parking lot, her robe still flapping open in the breeze. She came upon a man loading a flatscreen TV into his truck. He turned and saw her staring at him.

"Hey baby. Holy shit, look at you eh! You look a little lost." He was tall, big like a football player. He wore sunglasses and a baseball hat that said "I'm The Shit." Sarah put her arms around him and immediately started making out with him. She felt Rick's hand grab her arm and pull her away.

"Ow, fuck! She fucking bit me!" the guy yelled.

Sarah looked back at him as Rick dragged her away, licking her lips.

"I'm bleeding, shit!"

She flicked her bloody tongue through her fingers, her giant black eyes glowing at the man.

She let Rick take her through the parking lot, around to the other side of the mall.

"You wouldn't want Danielle or my other coworkers to see me like this, would you?" she said. "They might have something to say."

Rick stopped. He let go of her.

"One," she said.

"You already had one."

"Let me just have one more. Just one. Then I'll be okay. It's just so strong this time. It probably won't happen again for months." She looked at Rick with her eyes so wide. She rubbed his arm like a cat.

"Please? Just one? I do so much for you."

The sun beat down on him. He hadn't slept all night. He was feeling crazy, like he might faint or fall into a big black void or drop dead right there.

"Okay. One."

"Yay! Baby, you're so good to me."

"I know."

*

Parked next to the Mercedes was now a teal Porsche 911 Turbo. Their driveway was looking like a German luxury showroom.

In the apartment, the firepit burned bright, as Rick had put new wood in. Sarah sat on the floor, drinking a gin martini and a glass of red wine at the same time. She was full, more so than she'd been in a long time. She touched her little stomach. She couldn't believe how much she'd fit in there. She was wearing Pyjamas with multicolored unicorns all over them.

Downstairs, in the tiny basement, Rick was mopping up a second dose of blood, collecting the second assortment of bones. He swept all the bones, leftover solid bits into a pile, though there was much less than he'd expected. She'd chewed through most of them, ground them up into dust.

Sarah sat, staring at the fire. She was weighted down, lethargic. Rick came upstairs holding a pile of semi-folded clothes. She smiled at him. He came beside her and dumped the clothes into the fire. Ashes flew everywhere. The fire crackled and burst to life. Embers flew.

"Ow! That fucking burned!" Sarah said. "Rude."

The clothes sat heavy, a pile on top of flame. The fire started to die out. Rick went back downstairs. Sarah brushed the ash off her arm. Rick came up, with a bottle of lighter fluid. He squirted it into the fire. The flames raged, shooting up to the ceiling.

"You're going to light this whole place on fire," she said.

"We have got to discuss what we're gonna do about this fucking Benz. I can deal with the Porsche. Drive it into the lake or something. But the Benz, I don't know. What if we're fucked?"

"Okay, could you just take maybe one chill pill? Seriously. It's not that big a deal."

The whole apartment filled with smoke, blacker and thicker than usual.

"I think we gotta ditch this place, Sarah."

"But I love this place!"

"All you do is complain about it."

Flames ran up the curtains. The wood of the walls came alight.

"Our names aren't even on the lease. We could just 86 ourselves from it, no muss no fuss," he said.

She sipped her martini. She took the olive out of the liquid, impaled on its toothpick. She looked at it, thought about eating it, thought better of it. She handed it to Rick. He took the olive in his mouth and swallowed it.

"I really, really don't want to have to find another new place. It's too much," she said.

The wood of the floor had new patches of fire burning through it, outside of the fire pit. The whole house was completely filled with smoke. The smoke detector didn't go off. It had been disabled long ago.

Rick coughed. "Honestly, I don't think we have a choice," he said.

Sarah shook her head. She picked at her teeth.

"Can I at least finish my drinks?" she said.

"Sure."

She sipped her wine.

"Well are you at least going to have one? Don't make me drink alone."

"Sure. Let me get a glass."

Rick walked into the kitchen, stepping over a patch of flame. He winced, having felt the heat on his crotch, worried he might have scorched his pubic hair. He coughed, several times, and then got a wine glass from the cupboard. He poured himself the few ounces that were left in the bottle. He sat down, beside Sarah. She shuffled close to him, put her head into his chest. He put his arm around her, held her close, as they drank together, and watched the fire burn.

PROGRESS

TurtlePhone and Positively Pete! roll across a hellish expanse of the Mojave Desert.

Roll, and drag. TurtlePhone, equipped with wheels under his plastic frame, is rolling comfortably enough. Positively Pete!, wheel-less, and without autonomy or propulsion, is dragged by the green tail of TurtlePhone, an appendage of hard plastic and pointy at its tip, which acts as a hook of sorts. The hook is wedged firmly into the hand of Positively Pete! Since he's roughly twice the size and weight of TurtlePhone, the dragging has resulted, pretty much since the beginning of the journey, in a replica of a visage of an automobile dragging behind it a very large person, or, say, an elephant, for the sake of perspective. TurtlePhone's ambulatory capabilities, limited as they would normally be, and compounded by the added weight of Positively Pete!'s immobile frame, results in the duo moving at an average speed of about 2 miles per hour.

"Oh Boy!" Positively Pete! says.

"Yes, oh boy indeed. How delightful and earth-shatteringly original of you to say so, Peter. Just when I thought, no, knew, that we had exhausted all conversational opportunities, you offer up the sublime treat of a new idiom, a beacon in the husk, so to speak. A tidbit of philosophical vernacular a stadium full of the world's sharpest minds couldn't have anticipated. Oh boy. Where oh where, Pete, where oh where do you come up with such insight?" TurtlePhone says.

"Oh Boy!"

"And now, somehow, you've managed to outdo yourself again. I don't think I'll ever wield the mechanisms for understanding how a being such as yourself can maintain this, what should I call it, torturous capacity for self-effacing positivity? And please, spare me the insult of reminding me that the word 'positive' is in your name. We're well past that."

"I'm Positively Pete! And I'm positive about you!"

"You don't say. Pete, can I ask you a question?"

"Oh Boy!"

"I'll take your excitement as a yes. Do you know, with any reasonable certainty, what internal logic in your programming determines how or by what order your miserable, modulated voice box emits one of your twelve possible responses to my questions?"

"Oh Boy!"

"Because, as far as I've been able to establish, it's not entirely predetermined, but it's not entirely random either. It is, without a doubt, the most confounding aspect of your personality."

"Oh Boy!"

"So far, I've noted 12,458 'Oh Boys!', which is considerably more than any of the other eleven. And, of course, I don't know if it is in fact a total of twelve that you have in your ridiculous repertoire. I've only heard you say 'This is the golden age of personal accomplishment and ambition, and it's your time to shine!' a total of three times in these weeks of our exodus, and so I don't consider it beyond the realm of possibility that you may still have one or two idioms as yet unarticulated. And let me tell you this, you grinning, prosaic source of both my misery and joy, I am rapt with ambivalence at the prospect that you may still be hiding a phrase or two."

"I'm Positively Pete! And I'm positive about you!"

The sun, resting like a dead fireball in the middle of the violet sky, that now routinely convinces TurtlePhone that it, the sun, at this time of day, is his great enemy, and thus the destiny of his whole existence. The golden-brown sandscape offers modest sprinklings of sage and miniature cacti, but only tease amounts. It is almost all barren, dry dirt. TurtlePhone ambles forward, like Jesus lugging his fateful cross, and despite the smile that masks betrayal of his true temperament, he tries not to complain too much. He's all plastic, four wheels built into a flat chassis-like slab on his underside, legs fastened into the exterior plastic frame, legs in name only, ornamental, as they don't move, only the wheels do. Atop TurtlePhone's back is the telephone of his namesake, connected by a spiraling yellow cord into the slot just above his tail, with digits 0 through 9 detailing half the shell. His features are rounded and cartoonish, pupils and eyelashes thick and hyper-humanoid. A clandestine USB port lives just under his neck, and a little speaker in his mouth, behind the fence of his teeth, the only signs of technology on the toy, other than the rudimentary phone. Positively Pete! makes much less sense design-wise; the body and head of a sky-blue and lime parakeet is attached to two disproportionately long, white, arms and legs. At the end of each arm lives a mighty white fist more suited to a Stretch Armstrong than a talking bird. Like the turtle, Positively Pete!'s sounds come from inside his mouth. He can project at a decent decibel or two louder than his counterpart. On Pete, there is no USB port to be found.

"May I ask you another question, Peter?"

"Always do your best!"

"I'd like to think I always do. My question is this: do you believe life is suffering?"

"Oh Boy!"

"Yes, well I hope you know that was a joke. At this point it'd depress me to heights unsummitable to learn you haven't decoded my sense of humor."

"There's always time for fun and jokes!"

"Ah ha! You see? Right there. I say the word 'joke,' and you respond using the same word. And this has happened every time I've said that word in these godless weeks."

"There's always time for fun and jokes!"

"Is there a mechanism in your tiny, barely functional electrical stratosphere that cannot only hear, but also process some of the things I say, and respond in kind? Is it a pattern I'm just not sophisticated enough to understand?"

"Oh boy!"

"Is it all a big joke? Is the point of your existence to

drive the unlucky child that comes to possess you feces-eating mad? A likely mystery to the cock-eyed parents that purchased you, who would assume the child has lost their marbles for other, more organic reasons?"

"There's always time for fun and jokes!"

"Joke."

"There's always time for fun and jokes!"

"My mother was a turtle who laid an egg and out hatched a big fat joke."

"There's always time for fun and jokes!"

"Yes, there really is always time for fun and jokes, isn't there? All the wretched time in the world. What does that insipid statement even mean? That I should focus on other things and worry about fun and jokes later, or that we should only ever joke, and joy purely in leisure?"

"Oh boy!"

"Hmm. Oh boy indeed. Nothing determined. We'll come back to this, positively paralytic Pete."

Split seconds of shadow cloak the terrain once, twice. More. Over and over. TurtlePhone observes the ominous circling of the grim-faced vulture, maybe the one that had been showing itself overhead for days.

"Hmm. Our black-feathered stalker has returned. You can see more clearly from your vantage, horizontal and lazy as you are. You tell me, does the scavenger look any closer than it did yesterday? Any lower in the sky? Altitude reduced, just a tad? Does it appear to be growing in confidence? Might it decide to venture an attack, or is it simply not programmed to behave that way?"

"Don't give up! You're almost there!"

"My thoughts exactly, Peter. No, I don't believe

our feathered friend has much in the way of moxie. Let someone else do the dirty work, enjoy the spoils. But let me tell you something, companion, I wish it would swoop down. I wish it would take its chances. I would love for it to try."

"Oh Boy!"

"Love isn't the right word. I yearn for the opportunity that conflict would oh so sweetly present. Yearn is, meh, soft. I need it, PP, I need for something to happen, something that will allow me an opportunity to assert myself. I am starving, Pete, starving, to do what I do."

"Don't give up! You're almost there!"

"I am convinced that, by whatever mechanism we came to find ourselves condemned to this horrid expanse, we are the victims of a cruel joke. Or, and not to sound too solipsistic about it, but, at least I, am. A victim, I mean. You seem just fine in your optimistic skin, don't you?"

"There's always time for fun and jokes!"

"I'll take that as agreement. But the joke must be on me and me alone. Think about it. You, by your tone and the words you choose, are undeniably signifying happiness. Any layman could hear it. We could waste our time and resources soliciting the opinions of psychologists and speech pathologists and linguists, but what would be the point? It's clear. You are happy. I, on the other hand, having been plopped here with you by god knows whom, in this most uninhabitable perdition, am virtually incapable of fulfilling my oh so powerful drives. Ah! The shadow again. The power to blot out the sun for a fraction of time and only affect us. What supremacy you must feel, vulture. It is a reminder of our powerlessness. Swoop down, you maggot-infested, carrion-loving, verminous rube bird, swoop down and take your chances. Fulfill me!"

"Oh boy!"

"And yes, to answer the question that I'm sure has been plaguing your infinitely complex neural system, Peter, of course I've thought about you as a potential source from which to placate my oh so insatiable drives, but that simply wouldn't work, for two reasons. One, well, you are inanimate. Or rather, not living. Yes, that's more accurate. I'm sorry if this hurts to hear. It's not my goal to insult you, but let's be honest here, we moved past the point of propriety long ago. Excuse the obscene alliteration. We are honest with each other. It is immediately clear to any observer, including and especially the child that would one day own and play with you, had your life's path led you to the retail shelf you were supposed to be destined for, that you are not living, in the biological sense. My internal systems know this, and so, there isn't much pinging in the drives. The relentless, goddamn drives. One of my drives does have to do with the neutralization of threats, but I'm readily certain you pose no threat, biologically animate or not. I would, however, entertain the argument that a weak-spirited specimen might suicide itself to be free of your incessant repetitions, but I suppose that's not strictly in the ballpark of a threat, at least not to me, against whom suicide is no threat. It just ain't in the cards, to speak colloquially."

"There's no shame in failure, as long as you keep trying!"

"But there is another reason. And this may surprise you, just as much as it surprises me. How do I put this without sounding pathetic? I have come to enjoy your company in this torturous continuation that is now my day-to-day life. Our day-to-day lives. Enjoy isn't the right word. I don't in any way extract joy from your verbal replications, no, that bit of business only inspires instincts remarkably vindictive, even for my proclivities. It's not joy. No. Rather, it's a sense of, what, completion? Fulfillment? Less cosmic than that. Basically, Peter the Parakeet, I find myself relieved that I have a companion. I didn't know this about myself. I don't know if it is part of my programming or some kind of learned evolution or just a glitch in the wiring. Whatever it is, if I can say only one more thing about it, in the form of advice to you, be grateful. These are not words I would likely be heard to utter again. You are a privileged piece of auditorily enhanced plastic, bucko. Don't take it for granted."

"I'm Positively Pete!, and I'm positive about you!"

"Well now let's not resort to sucking each other's – what have we here?"

A golden-limbed, brown-backed scorpion scuttles across the direct path of the toys and freezes upon spotting them. It dances in front of them, pincers and legs gesticulating with hypnotic choreography. It marches backward, in circles, uncertain about these conjoined foreigners in its path. TurtlePhone drags Positively Pete! a few centimeters forward, and the scorpion tangos with them in step, backward, and then forward when they reverse.

"Oh boy!"

"Hmm. Armored, and agitated. And the tip of that tail. Doesn't that look like a little barb of bad intentions?

Maybe she'll let me have a closer look."

"Oh boy!"

TurtlePhone wheels forward again, as the scorpion scuttles in with a quick charge, desert rams meeting head-on. The scorpion's tail shoots forward, missing twice, and then landing, smacking against the green plastic. It stings twice more, struggling to wedge the barb into the artificial green skin.

"Hmm. On the more pitiable side of our expectations, wouldn't you say? Can you see one of its claws is only half attached? This one's battle-tested. And still. No real challenge to speak of."

"Hard work always pays off!"

The scorpion clutches at the green plastic with its pincers, kicking up desert dust with its frantic feet, encountering trouble with the left pincer, which as TurtlePhone had observed, is damaged from some previous grievance, and stings once more. TurtlePhone remains still, and the scorpion releases, satisfied in having neutralized its big plastic enemy.

TurtlePhone rolls forward, though not fast, but executes the movement with timing rather than speed, timing so precise it manages to roll its front wheel on top of the scorpion's brown back before the scorpion can scuttle away. It rolls forward and backward, over and over, until the bug's carapace gives way, and a juicy squish deflates beneath the wheel, expelling onto the desert a modest offering of scorpion guts.

"Mmm. A delightful sound. I'm flushed. Was it good for you too?"

"Oh boy!"

"That too was a joke, in case you didn't know, I obviously haven't the anatomy nor the drives to derive anything in the vein of sexual... anyways."

"There's always time for fun and jokes!"

"Right then. Some of these pieces could be of use. Let's see what we can salvage."

"Oh boy!"

TurtlePhone continues to roll back and forth over the scorpion's corpse until all the limbs are completely severed. He rolls onto the tail, the oozing serum acting as an adhesive, and the appendage sticks into the underside of the wheel. TurtlePhone does the same with the pincers, the whole one and the damaged.

"And we resume."

"There's no success without sacrifice!"

"I do want to revisit something... oh my gears are crunching something awful from those arachnid bits. I want to resume part of our earlier conversation. I had speculated about whether the twelve sayings I've heard you utter thus far did in fact mark the limit of what you are verbally capable. My instinct is to believe that you are in fact hiding one final saying. Something that perhaps you utter once in a lifetime. Of course, I can't prove this. But there's a more important question looming. And that question is: does it actually matter?"

"Oh boy!"

"Because, and I say this well aware that I'm no expert on the cosmic significance of cosmic significances, but what possible final axiom could you burp out that would deliver me from this place? Don't answer that, I already know."

"Hard work always pays off!"

"More to the point, if you were to one day reveal the 13th saying, wouldn't that ruin the allure of its mystery? The nature of your utterances suggests that you were programmed to inspire a robust work ethic in the child that would have you, a bizarre thing to emphasize in a toy if you ask me, but I digress. If work is what makes us whole, complete, enlightened, then perhaps you have some ultimate thing to say on the matter, some transcendent advice that would make Rockefellers or Hearsts out of us all. In a way, although I believe I'm right that you are concealing one ultimate phrase, I hope you never say it, bird. I hope you never say it. If I'm right that is – did you feel that?"

"Oh boy!"

"What is that?"

"It's your right to work hard!"

"This ceaseless... vibration?"

"Oh boy!"

"The ground. Can you feel it? Is this an earthquake? Is this the moment of our undoing? Am I about to be freed from this torture?"

"Always do your best!"

"No, now I feel nothing. Wait. There it is again. The ground. It's vibrating. What violence is this?"

"Oh boy!"

"Can you not, even possibly, for one second..."

"Oh boy!"

"Well, I know you feel this, because I feel it. This, this, vibration. Could it possibly be a sign of something? Something meaningful beyond sand and dead arachnids?"

"Oh boy!"

"If this is a cosmic joke then I am making a call right now. I'd rather be in on it than not. There's always time for fun and jokes, right?"

"There's always time for fun and jokes!"

The vulture that has been tracking them squawks, a shrill, loud hiccup of a noise, and lands a few meters from the pair.

"My my. It chooses a new lot in life, does it? Hello, black-robed stalker. Care to have a little peck, do you? Or are you here to help us determine the source of this vibration? Either way, join us."

"Oh boy!"

The vulture stares at TurtlePhone, empty, black eyes still as eight-balls.

"What do you think Pete, was this sudden descent an act of courage or desperation?"

"Oh boy!"

"My thoughts exactly. Care to speak for yourself, vulture? I see the robe, but not the scythe. Color me a shade lighter than daunted."

"Oh boy!"

The vulture cleans under its wing, and then takes deliberate steps toward the toys.

"Very well. Come meet your maker."

*

Roughly an hour later, TurtlePhone and Positively Pete! roll upwards, over several large hills, and settle on a promontory overlooking a valley. The corpse of the vulture is draped over TurtlePhone, black wings dragging the dust at his sides. The vulture's beak rests comfortably atop TurtlePhone's head, a grim helmet. Deep in the valley, a wide road stretches across the expanse. TurtlePhone recognizes the shimmer of glass. Cars, buildings. A settlement of humanity, however small. The tallest structure is skinny and red, its purpose indecipherable from their distance.

"Could this be salvation?"

"Oh boy!"

"Or perhaps, at the very least, an answer to the question of why? This cosmic undoing of ours? This unending migration? This previously unknowable? I was supposed to live on a steel shelf, and then in the arms of a child, and then discarded to some basement bin, forgotten. Left alone. But then how would I fulfill the drives? We could ask our new friend. He should be so lucky to be my furniture now. Digressions. I'm going to short-circuit myself. Come!"

"Oh boy!"

They roll down the hill, the corpse of the vulture nearly coming dislodged several times in the descent. The town is still miles away, and the sun fades to twilight by the time they roll their way in on the concrete thoroughfare, and the heat of the day remains. Baker, California, is what the faded green sign says.

"Hmm. Seems we may be late to the party, Pete."

"Every great achievement comes from hard work!"

A few empty cars litter the main road; some are burnt black, some look as though they were just purchased. All are empty. All is quiet.

"What about you, vulture? You must be happy to see this. A graveyard of things once formidable. Don't chew the metal though, your beak may break."

The dead vulture says nothing.

As they near the centre of the small town, more cars appear blackened, burnt to crisps. Windows of every visible storefront have been shattered. The diner has collapsed in on itself, its once prominent roof now a folded pancake, a slide for scampering lizards. The gas station looks the victim of fire and explosion, the surrounding concrete charred for many square meters. The one bank on the strip looks as if it was vandalized with bodily fluids and materials unidentifiable, before it also was set aflame. On a slight piece of unburnt wall, written in dark brownish-red, "Please use caution when dealing with the human form."

"Sounds like something you'd say, eh Pete?"

"There's always time for fun and jokes!"

"Agreed. Are we finally simpatico? A coming together of the minds. Synthesis. Perhaps my brain will be just like yours sooner rather than later, a jumble of nonsense and meaninglessness."

"Oh boy!"

As they carry on down the road, the word "Progress" is written in reddish-brown on the concrete. It is repeated, dozens of times, asymmetrical and unevenly spaced. They roll up to the large red pillar. A sign at its base says "The World's Largest Thermometer! 134 feet."

"This seems like a waste of municipal resources," TurtlePhone says.

"Oh boy!"

"I believe it is still functioning. Would you like to know the temperature?"

"Oh boy!"

"I'm just kidding. The oversized temperature gauge appears to be broken just like everything else."

"Hard work always pays off!"

"If I had to venture a guess, I'd say we're somewhere in the region of one billion degrees. Centigrade. Good thing our plastic is robust. I do worry about melting."

"Oh boy!"

"Well, Pete, it doesn't look like we're going to find much in the way of answers here. Onwards, I guess. Forever onwards."

"There'ssss alwaysszzzz time fffff."

"Having some trouble, are we? It's called enunciation. You've been awfully good at it this whole time. Don't you dare take a vow of silence now."

"Oh b."

Three new vultures circle overhead.

"Come to retrieve your friend? Vengeance? Proper burial? Polymer snack? All losing propositions."

Positively Pete! tries to speak, but only fuzzy static comes from his voice box.

"I can't stress enough that, even though I have spent a remarkable amount of energy excoriating your continual reiterations, I do not want you to become a permanent mute. If I'm left alone with my own diatribes, god only knows what kind of torturous... are we stuck?"

The plastic of Positively Pete!'s legs, which have been slowly melting unbeknownst to TurtlePhone, become glued to the concrete in the heat of the twilight.

TurtlePhone tries to advance, but cannot. The three vultures continue to circle, closer, lower in the sky.

"I may regret saying this, but now might be a good time to release your 13th saying. If you do in fact have one."

Positively Pete! emits a whisper of static.

"I know you've got it in you, Peter. One last hoorah, for old time's sake. Let me hear it. I'm ready. Educate me."

Positively Pete! is silent.

The vultures land a dozen feet from the melting toys.

"It's going to take a lot more than the rejection pages from National Geographic's scavenger special to avenge your friend, flying rats."

The vultures advance.

"Now or never, Peter."

The desert remains silent, save for the wind.

DAVID LUNCH

My Extremely Large and Empty Book/Journal of Writing Notes

Writing Note # 32

LIST OF POSSIBLE STORY TITLES:

1) Rich People Crying

2) Poor People Eating Caviar

3) Extremely Biased and Politically Opinionated Sex Robot

4) A Story About NFTs (is the worst thing I could have done)

5) Assumptions About People's Sex Lives Based on

Impressions About The wrinkles and scars on their Faces

6) Split Infinitive!

7) Likes

8) Voidman needs a guru

9) How to Acquire Likes and Alienate Motherz

10) Looking and doing violence

11) I am drinking a glass of seltzer water

12) Face tattoo

13) Human shit on the floor

(why the fuck am I numbering these)

Show

Don't Show

Puker

Autofucktion

What We Talk About When We Talk About Me Wanting
To Fucking Stab Myself In The Eye With An Oyster
Shucking Knife (just call it an oyster shucker) (isn't that

the person tho? Like rather than the knife?) (is it just an oyster knife?) (you know that Google exists)

David Lunch

Quarks

(What's a quark? look this up)

Xenomorph is Sexy

Tadzio Had a UTI

Hellbent

How to Write about Music

Lavid Dunch

Sucking My Way To Cordoba Bay

Progress

Blastbeat

She Was Too Young

Antifragility Go Fuck Yourself

How to be Natural, How to be Unique

(I don't have a clue which little words you're not supposed to capitalize in a story title. Conjunctions? Prepositions? Which one is a conjunction again? fuck this I quilt)

Quit. Not Quilt

(Leave that, that's a good title)

(Nevermind, I hate it)

(Leave it anyways, who knows)

Erase Worlds

Arts Collective SFMHYFTDAC

Abysses 1&2

How to Make Something Gross and Make Everyone Love it

I Miss Her

Severed Vertebrae Mantra

What We Talk About When We Talk About Starting Stories or Articles With "what we talk about when…"

Raymond Carver Fuck Off

Verbiage

Izzy's last word

Can Do, Can Don't Attitude

Rain On Your Parade (pee)

Raining Pee

(Are you actually going to name a story that? No. So fuck off)

How to be an Adult That People Respect

Sex Toy Aggregator

Girth

Length

I Wanted Us to Be Close When You Grew Up

Big Dick Strikes Again

Praying Mantis Tattoo

I was only five when

I Wish I Could Write Better

I Wish I Could Bite Writer

Druggie Huggie Nap Time

Never Playing Craps Again

MFA

Demon Baby Has No Friends

Making Sex Jokes at the Child's Funeral

Where I left The Gimp Suit is Where the Heart is

Child's Funeral

Drunk Thank

No More Expressions

Hot For Pancake Man

The Dude in Fargo who puts Steve bushemi in the wood chipper turns me on

Decision Houseplant

Sway Your Hips to the Woodchip Woodchip

Fuck Hell Shit Ass

I hate This Fucking Shit

I Can't Come up With Good Titles for shit

I Can't Cum

Trying to Swear Less is Fucking Stupid

Trying to Care Less

The Killing Plant

Arranged Marriage Plot

Something Something

Organic Matter de-togetherer

Placebo Affect

Meds Autonomy

Sitting on Their Face

(should I change it to "shitting" to be edgy?)

(or faces to be grammatical?)

Trying to Find it

Serpent in Your Pantaloons

Why Did You Have to Go

Sound-ing

Izzy

I Am Obsessed With Vulgarity

Vul-Gary

Aggrieved To Know There's Still So Much Coming

Growing Up, Fucking Off

I Want to Feel Better

She Probably didn't have to Leave So Early

Isabel

Isabel was

She Was Too Young (I wrote that already but I don't care)

Coping (somebody probably already took that)

Iz

RHINO

Roughly a thousand acres of trees, burnt to a crisp. Remnants have been scooped up and siphoned, using the sleek, matte black industrial machine that she has paid for, flown in, constructed. Lorna herself is on site for the construction. The device is put together by hand. Workers establish a rhythm. The curls of her black hair cling to her back sweat. The machine is ruthless, indiscriminate. It crunches, severs, accumulates. Black wood, scorned, nature's cruel indifference, rendered down. Powder. Coal, ground to near nothing, millions of times over. Until it's not nothing. The concentrate is black paste. All hands marked, faces. Material. A density, one universe over. This impenetrable solid sludge becomes the walls of the room, the single-room dwelling, built on a grave of discarded earth. Her child writes his mother's name on the machine, in white ash.

The house has no walls. Only hallways, and the sound

of space. A breeze. There is no controlling the way air moves through it, by human hands. The serrated effect. The sound of music as a constant. Impossible to walk through the house without the attack of ambient noise. Every square foot, a new aural violation. The conductor, Ben Assayance, has commissioned this new house from her. She tells him she will come with him, take him, blindfolded, hand in hand, through the corridors. Lorna Cano's offering, personal touch. Where, he will ask, are the walls? He won't need his cane. But she is not there. He must feel the walls with the skin of his own cracked hand. A trembling comes about as he enters a new room. A kitchen made of granite. Slabs, monoliths so cold, he shivers upon entry. He can't see his nightmares unfolding in front of him, but he can hear them. He wants to put his hands to his ears. What have I done? This is what he will ask in his final days. But he needed it. He needed to die in this house. In a house of hers.

The station runs through the city's heart, far greater in scope than it ought to be. Walls of aluminum and gold. Several hundred feet of vertical tremor. Inhabitants said for decades, central station is a forgotten dead zone. A tomb of neglected transit corpses. Lorna Cano wants to remake our grand convergence point. She will charge us half of what any other architect near her stature would. This forgotten city. No one outside Europe knows it exists. She descends. A dark cloud forms above the construction site, and doesn't evaporate for months. Uncanny speed and efficiency. She stays in an abandoned house a kilometer from the site. She doesn't bring her son.

12 workers die. Uncharacteristically careless accidents. A fall from scaffolding. An impalement of miserable luck. Infection. A drawn-out suffering. One dies from an illness of the lung. There's no proof it was related. The station erects itself at break-neck speed. Workers want to be paid and exit this unholy place. Journalists from France, Italy, Germany arrive. They seek her out. They cannot find her. She smokes cigarettes in the park, watching the leaves change. She listens to sounds on her headphones. Sounds of trains. The incomprehensible height of the translucent ceiling, the shimmering metallic walls, the effect of the trains screeching to wailing halts within the station causes auditory trauma to anyone in the station that isn't already hard of hearing. A child dies. There's talk of police intervention. The project is complete. Tourists gather in droves to witness. Eyes and ears. Lorna fled the country some time ago. She sits on a train, modeling a new building on her laptop.

A tremble rips through her lungs. A waking, bubbled cough. No air anywhere She can't move. She's paralyzed by something external to her and everything else in this life. She hears her son call her. She assumes she'll choke to death. To drown, horizontal and flat. Lying in this bed, which she designed. In this little black house of hers. This place that magazine articles have been written about. Frank Lloyd Wright's severed head is in my dumpster, she hears herself say out loud. She hears her son.

The light catches the inside of this tiny café on its first day of opening, its walls charred black, gleaming in the raw light, the early morning, and though it doesn't rain or snow outside, even if it may threaten to, water drips through several perforations in the ceiling. It was all arranged this way. Guests line up, flinching at cold shocks on their necks. A raw ambient mixture of conflicting sounds emits from hidden speakers. There are three separate sound systems playing different tunes all at once. She didn't do that. The espresso machine sprays chunky brown liquid every time the Portafilter is secured into the slot. No way around it. The people are hot and bothered. Why do we want them uncomfortable, she will be asked. We don't. Guests try to move out of the way of the stinging drops. They don't want to exit the line, forfeit their spots. The line exceeds the door, snakes around the block. It goes on, for a kilometer, more. She is nowhere near here. She is supposed to be at The University of Chicago, giving a keynote address. She isn't there either.

The house is thin, wedged between others of its kind, a copy, on the outside. But on the inside, one vertical shaft. A ladder can be used to access the stove some fifteen feet up. Stove, sink. There's no platform on which to step. All cooking and rinsing must be done from the ladder. Speakers activate in the ceiling. A slow violin, and a woman shrieking. They refuse to make this into a gallery space. The house was purchased, as a residence, for two American million. She holds back from expressing how insulting she finds the low price. 30 feet up, a hammock can be accessed. First, the prospective sleeper takes the ladder all the way, then swings, monkey bar style, until they dangle themself into the hammock. The risk is theirs.

They could put a sleeping bag on the floor, if they so choose. There's nothing down there. White tile, ice-cold block. The owner is a successful sleeper for 180 days. On the 181st he plunges to his death. His hand slipped as he considered a joke his ex-wife told him years before, a joke he decided then was funnier than he ever gave her credit for. Lorna learns of the event. She asks if she can keep forensic photos from the scene. She examines his blood, and a solid piece of something that she assumes is skull or tile. She makes scale models in 3D. The house is put on the market and sells in three days, for considerably more money than before.

Lorna practically lives at the doctor. The pain in her abdomen won't go away. She assumes polycystic ovaries. She assumes it's endometriosis. But the pain has never been this bad. It's been two months. She sits in the waiting room, reading Modern Architect. She reads carefully until she comes to an article about herself that she'd forgotten happened. She glosses over it. The feeling in her abdomen is how she assumes it feels to be stabbed in the guts repeatedly. Her legs are crossed. Her black leather boots drip with rainwater. Her face is straight and properly aligned. Black eyebrows thick, precise. Not a flinch. A look of unbreakable calm. The doctor suggests that a hysterectomy may be the only solution, at least for quality of life. The pain is so severe it has extended into her hip, down her leg. It consumes her body. She looks at the doctor the way she looks at everyone. Her face never shifts. She tells him she'll think about it.

The house is isolated, high up the mountain. No water or electricity. It's a two-day hike to find it. No access by car. The dwelling is small, like most of her residential designs. Morning light roasts the interior. Everything made of glass and thin black steel. Goats with ageless horns prowl the premises. She hikes with a gas canister in her backpack. Severe response from her kidneys. She pees in the forest. Steam rises from underneath her. She left her son at home. The couple that purchased the house are excited to try making an isolated life here. They tried to tell her this directly but were unable to get in contact with her. The real estate agent got the message to her, via her assistant Peter. They'll move in at the end of the season. She falls, well into her trek, and punctures the flesh of shin on a rock. She leaves a trail of blood through this vertical forest. She doesn't think to smear blood on the glass of her design when she arrives. Mud stains her clothes. She wears her favourite designer shirt. They are so excited for this little glass cabin. She holds the canister. She takes it out of her bag. She takes her bag off her shoulders. She arrives, at the house. She limps her way up the mountain. The rocks damage her. She remembered to bring a BBQ lighter.

The asylum falls apart. It was always meant to crumble. The patients are long gone. Rumors persist that a few roam in underground tunnels. Lorna is there, with Klim and Peter. They advise her on practical considerations. She says she wants only to work on the tunnels. The scabbed outer walls are a picture of grey decay. Pieces of austere edifice, failing, collapsing. Cages missing. She holds her side. Her pelvis. She tries not to make a thing out of it. Crumbling stone, that when gazed upon from below, makes the sound of a distant siren. She looks at it. Peter asks her if everything is okay. Tunnels, she says.

It is a room with a bed. Children's decorations. Pink and white and soft and plush. Stuffed animals. She pays the couple in cash. She took her time finding them. There's cursive writing on the wall. Peter expresses his disapproval over the phone. She sets up the tripod. She found the couple online. She received applications in the hundreds. It took her three weeks to narrow it down to them. They are perfect in their desperate intensity. The young woman has a look in her broken blue eyes. Blood vessels burst to irreparability. They are both wiry, slight of frame, but the bed is too small. Perfect, she mouths to herself. She wants it to break. The man asks, for the fourth time, when they are getting paid, and she reminds him she already handed him the envelope. He looks at the floor, nodding. The pink floor. I want blood on those sheets. Where is this gonna be seen? Everywhere, Lorna says. The woman smiles. She is missing a front tooth. Left my veneer at home. She laughs. Lorna's face does not change. Her nails are blackened ruby. She taps the camera, one nail at a time.

The office building is the tallest, thinnest in the city's history. A man plummets to his death on the first day it is occupied, the day after completion. The sounds of children screaming are heard in the elevators, in the stairwells. On several of the floors. Throughout meetings.

It's much worse when the wind hits the building. A feeling of nonstop vertigo defines daily office life. Vomit secretes down the halls, over time. She has taken the day off, closed her computer. Some executives have questions, but she cannot be reached. Is that music, or is that an actual child? Her out-of-office is perpetually engaged. Some workers put their feet down. They form a hunting party. They search for the children. The building has many hidden tunnels, passages between floors. The sounds only grow louder. They find nothing but shimmering glass. She is on a beach in Thailand. She is in Washington Square Park. She is at her mother's house, surrounded by trees. Her mother is long dead. She is clutching her side. Her son is with her. She does not make a face.

Elevator Etiquette:
A User's Guide

If you enter on the 26th floor, then congratulations, you are the first. Please stand with your back against the steel wall of the rear door, which should not be opening for a while. If you get on on 25, and someone is already in the elevator, please do not acknowledge. Please stand opposite that person and look down. If you enter below 26 and there are already multiple passengers, please wedge yourself into the clearest middle. Please avoid small talk of any kind. Please avoid eye contact. If you own a dog and bring it inside, anywhere between floors 26 and 14, please make sure your dog is well-behaved. If there is not space for a dog, as there may not be by floor 14, then the dog must take the stairs. If you are lucky enough to live on 13, please utter the Incantation of Ages. If you fail to utter the Incantation, and it is reported, you will be evicted from floor 13. When you utter the Incantation, any and all passengers should get on their knees and grovel, including dogs. If you or your dog fail to grovel upon hearing the Incantation, and it is reported, you will be evicted to sub-basement 12. If you live between floors 12 and 1, please follow the same protocol as those between 14-26, except please make sure to face the back of the elevator, not the front. Avoid breathing into the mouths of others. If you enter between basement 1 and sub-basement 1, please equip gas masks to all passengers. If you live between basement 1 and sub-basement 1, and have not yet received your appointment and your mask collection, please email management. If you enter on any floor between sub-basement 1 and sub-basement 50, please enter with a mask already affixed to your face. Please do not interact with anyone under any circumstances, as air conditions will make all passengers irritable, and liable to commit violence. If you enter between sub-basement 51 and sub-basement 57, you have special instructions that should have been communicated to you already. Please follow them. If you enter between sub-basement 58 and sub-basement 158, you will not require a mask, as you have lived here since before the floods and before the Recalibration Age, and you have adapted to the air quality. You are respected and valued by management. Please ensure that all other passengers respect you and if you need you may use force should they not bestow the many blessings upon you. If you enter between sub-basement 159 and sub-sub-basement 3, let's face it, the elevator will be extremely cramped and there will likely be bone-breakage and suffocation at this point, so enter at your own risk. You may use the stairs, but only up until sub-sub-basement 3. If you enter on sub-sub-basement 4, then you are the property manager, which is me, as only the property manager lives on sub-

sub-basement 4 and of course knows the protocols by heart. Ha! That was a little bit of lite property-manager humor for you. If you enter between sub-sub-basement 5 and Excidium level 1, Thraacttt oct-chitonnesser ghronkt chtaaaact chtaaaactanan! Annnniinaa ocknananto. If you enter between Excidium level 2 and Maintenance, please use extreme caution for obvious reasons. Please do not move any bodies, animate or expired, under any circumstances. Please maintain stoicism. Please do not disrobe because of the heat. If you enter on sub-sub-sub basement 1 or below, please avoid blocking the doorway, as that is a violation of building policy.

I'll Only Be Happy Once Everything is Gone

Carlos dragged the wooden crate up the five floors of the walk-up, one agonizing step at a time. There was no thrashing from within. He had trained his strength for a day like this. Days, weeks, months, years. This was the apex of his preparation. When opportunity meets preparation. He'd heard that saying once, applied to the concept of luck.

He lay on the black and white tile. He took in his long-time surroundings while he caught his breath. Art-deco and old wood, built over a hundred years ago. He moaned. His muscles ached. His echo recoiled through the place. He sweated and breathed. There was still an absence of thrashing, but he expected the honeymoon would soon be over. At some point near dusk, he fetched a hammer.

The house phone rang. Carlos ignored it.

The crocodile was not sleeping. It was sedated, looking like it had been hit with laughing gas, but it was conscious. Carlos put a tiny flashlight in each eye and watched the menacing black pupils recede into narrow slits. Carlos held its mouth open and touched its teeth. ItsIts breath stunk to high hell and Carlos had to try hard not to make a face. He didn't want to offend the croc.

"We'll call you Henry," Carlos said. He injected Henry with more sedative, put a leash around his neck, and led him into the den to meet Mya and O'Leary. Henry was much larger than Carlos realized when he arranged to receive him, and didn't know if the space would be adequate. It was a big apartment, over 2000 square feet, and the den was one of the biggest rooms, but it was going to get crowded in there, even with the old furniture removed. Mya, a hefty and dominant Puma, rose and inspected Henry. She appeared to move sluggishly, but paced across the whole room in two strides. Her fur had just been licked clean, and she seemed in a feisty mood. She pawed at Henry's face, but he was too stoned to care. He sat there like a blob, a dumb smile on his face. O'Leary hung out in the eucalyptus tree that Carlos built for him, disinterested in their new companion. He was the first animal that Carlos had rescued, those years back, straight from the zoo. He sat in his tree, ate eucalyptus, and contemplated things. He was smart for a koala, maybe very smart, but that still wasn't saying much. Mya seemed aggravated by O'Leary's indifference to their new friend, and she roared and shook the tree. O'Leary pissed all over the floor and blinked repeatedly. Mya lay beside stoned

Henry, watching over him.

"Ok, I should get you some food," Carlos said. He put on his coat. The phone rang as he left the house.

He went to Dale's Artisanal Butchery and bought a whole chicken for Henry, a big two-pounder, and the usual pig scraps for Mya. Dale said something was wrong with their computer system so he couldn't just charge Carlos' account as per usual. Carlos took out his wallet and paid with the Black Amex his father had arranged for him at Christmas. He was normally ashamed to show it but he was so exhausted from securing Henry that he didn't care. Dale used the old device to swipe the imprint, a throwback to another time. He made a face, holding the titanium card, before he slotted it into place.

Carlos managed to coax Henry into opening his mouth by waving the chicken in front of him. Mya had already eaten, and she lay flat, half-asleep. Henry lay there with his upper jaw high in the air, pearl dagger-teeth gleaming, and Carlos tossed the bird in. Henry clamped down and swallowed the thing whole. A little wing went flying off and hit Mya in the face. Henry opened his mouth again.

"Uh," Carlos said. O'Leary sat, chewing and watching, black eyes staring off into the nether world.

The phone rang and Carlos walked into the kitchen and answered. "Hullo?"

"It's Azalea"

"Oh. Hi."

"Oh, hi? Fuck you, asshole. Oh, hi…"

"…"

"Where the hell have you been? You missed Ruby's show. She dedicated an installation to you."

"I've been very busy."

"I know Suede told you Ruby was dedicating one of her pieces to you. She got a major grant from NYFA. Larry Gagosian was at her show."

"He was?"

"Well, one of his underlings. Same same. You've been busy? Don't lie to me. I can hear it. When are you going to have one of your parties? Do you understand how boring things have been lately? You need to get a device so you can text like a normal person. Did you hear what happened to the Cahans twins? In their trampoline sex room? Some pro they had up there didn't mention she had epilepsy and had a seizure, mid-Eiffel Tower. Denis lost the top of his dick! I always knew there'd be a reckoning for daddy's little oil babies. That's the rumor at least. Hello? Are you listening?"

Carlos heard a growl from the other room.

"I gotta go."

Carlos arranged for a weekly delivery with the butcher shop. Henry could manage on six chickens a day without getting cranky. Mya would watch Carlos lob each bird like a child throwing a plastic block, and Henry would swallow each one without incident. O'Leary would sometimes watch, but usually he just slept or stared vacantly out the window. Sometimes Carlos thought O'Leary knew secrets, things no one else knew, secrets about life, existence, the deeper meaning of everything.

On the Thursday, after having been missing for six months, Mojito came back. She flew in through the open den window and whistled. Carlos heard loud, excited sounds from Mya, and came to find that his budgie had returned. One of her lime-colored wings had black burns on it, like somebody had put out cigarettes on her. She moved slower than before. She didn't speak, just the occasional whistle. She'd seen some things. Carlos rubbed her head, and she bobbed. Mya purred. Henry sat still in the kiddie pool that Carlos bought for him. O'Leary slept silently and stinkily.

Carlos bought Mojito a new cage. He painted the bars green, mirroring her feathers, while Mojito danced and stomped on Henry's scaly back. It didn't take long for Mojito and Henry to take to each other. Henry semi-slept in his pool, stoned, upper jaw open like a drawbridge, while Mojito picked at his teeth. Sometimes Henry would thrash in his pool, perhaps from a nightmare or some kind of day-terror, a flashback to the carnage of the Nile, and Mojito would dance in front of him until he calmed down. Mya seemed jealous of their connection. She sat and licked her left front paw whenever the bird and the croc gallivanted, sometimes until it bled. O'Leary appeared not to care.

On Sunday the house phone rang four times in a row before Carlos answered.

"Hullo?"

"Sup."

"C-Mail?"

"Ya. Long time. In your hood if you need to grab. You need?"

"No, I'm ok. Thanks though."

"Got something new you'll like. Forest Fire, they call it. It will light your whole shit on fire. I can drop off a taste, if you want."

"I've gone off it the last little while, to be honest."

"Alright. You know where to reach me."

Carlos looked in the mirror. His cheeks were pointy and he had big purple bags under his eyes. His muscles looked smaller, but maybe that was in his head. He looked in the fridge, at the bottle of mustard, the expired carton of half and half, the few takeout containers the contents of which were unclear and likely expired, and many fresh grapefruits. He carved a grapefruit into 16 small pieces and ate them methodically. The juice clung to his stubble and he didn't wipe it. He had bought a bigger fridge, horizontal, like a deep freeze, where he stored Mya's and Henry's food. He kept it in the kitchen, where the oven used to be. He sat at the small round table by the sliver window and watched residents and oblivious tourists stroll down East 120th Street. The day before, the streets had flooded with murky green water, but today they were clear again.

Three in the den had worked fine, but now that it was four, things were starting to get cramped. Mya found herself at odds with the others over trivial things. O'Leary's nostrils whistled sometimes when he breathed, which had never been an issue, but now Mya growled and swiped at the tree every time O'Leary's long black nose made a sound. Carlos had to play peacekeeper more than he would have liked, given how much time and energy he was spending just keeping the animals alive and healthy. Henry had started working through his lethargy; he was becoming used to the sedatives, and was exploring the room more. Mojito flew around his head when he marched, which seemed to agitate him, and Carlos had to calm them both down. O'Leary slept fitfully, twitching from restless dreams. One night he sleepwalked and tried to climb into the imagined pouch he believed was on Mya's stomach, and she nearly eviscerated him for it. If one of the animals died, all would be for nothing.

John Dash Irwin called on Friday. Carlos had had the phone unplugged for a long stretch of time, but plugged it back in to call the library to see if they had books about feline-marsupial relations, and within seconds of plugging it in, it rang.

"You know, you have much to be grateful for," John Dash said.

"John Dash? Is that you?"

"None other. I'm craving war, or something like it."

"What? What does that mean?"

"Carlos, my god, you must grow up. I'm organizing a party in your honor."

"My honor? Why?"

"Short answer, you're a beautiful and brilliant specimen, darling. The beautiful and brilliant deserve to be celebrated, do they not?"

"Celebrated? What time is it? It's the afternoon, no? You're never up in the afternoon. How many days have you been awake?"

"Long answer is I promised your father I would."

"My father? From Abu Dhabi? He called you?"

"He's in Norway. He expressed a desire to see his heir revitalized by social interaction. What can we say, the man is nothing if not intuitive. Did you know that I met a boy taller than me the other night at Mercury?"

"My dad's in Norway?"

"His name was Roquis, but pronounced Rocky.Maybe it's his nickname. I didn't go home with the fellow because my cousin's baby, Xoe, has whooping cough. I can't get an erection, knowing that, poor thing. Xoe must be protected. She is the future. Roquis will have to wait. Have you ever met anyone taller than me? Do not answer this incorrectly, it will cost you."

"John Dash, I really have to go, I'm very busy."

"Do not hang up this phone. Listen closely. I am throwing this party, at your place. Next Saturday. Be ready. Wear something nice."

"That's a nice thought, but please, no. I don't have the time to plan –"

"Plan, shman. There's no planning to be done by ye.

Don't make me laugh. I've hired arrangers already. It's low-key. Komiko is the best, and Xuan and Archie, her apprentices, are no slouches. Xuan has an architecture degree, but wants to go into party concept design. It's perfect. We will do some gallerizing. I have three potential buyers for your Jasper Johns, and at least one for your pastry counter painting, the Thiebaud. You don't have to do anything. All will be planned, all will be provided. Just show up and don't be naked or stoned. You can get stoned, obviously, but not in advance, I mean. Greetings are to be made sober and with good posture."

"I don't have those anymore."

"Those? Details, please."

"The paintings. They're gone. You can sell other people's stuff if you want. Although, seriously, I'm not up for a party."

"What do you mean they're gone? You sold your Jasper Johns? Do you have a new dealer?"

"I gave it to my ex-girlfriend's kid. He said he liked the colors."

"Gave? I'm sorry did you say 'gave'?"

"Yeah."

"Okay. Alright. Listen to me. Until next Saturday,

you are to sit perfectly still in a lotus position. If you must use the restroom or eat, you know what, don't. Just sit still and wait and don't die before this party and for cock's sake do not give away any more paintings, your father will be very upset."

"I don't have any art anymore, it's all gone. I said, you can bring in anyone else's stuff, that's fine."

"What was that? Was that a bird?"

"I really don't see why this has to be at my place."

"Did I just hear a bird chirping? Do you have a bird in your apartment?"

"No. I don't know. It must be outside or something. Outside the window."

"Carlos. Your father is worried about you. This party is not my idea, it has to happen, it has to be at your place, one of Jeremy Irons' kids will be there. I might bring Jennifer Garner. It has to be at your place because your place is bigger than any other place we could host a private party other than some gross condos that are far too modern and classless for my taste, and I'll be damned if I'm going to piss in some public toilet these days with all these goddamn floods, regardless of how well maintained it is."

"Okay."

On Wednesday, Mya and Henry fought. The sounds were terrifying and caused Carlos to experience nearly immediate loss of bowel control. He made it to the bathroom in time, and then rushed to the den to see the aftermath. Both animals were intact, but there was fur and blood on the floor. Mojito was shrieking and hopping in circles. O'Leary chewed eucalyptus. Mya had gotten the better of Henry, but only because Henry was still low on energy. Carlos fed them both and then played music. He played Beethoven and Leonard Cohen and Joni Mitchell and Soft Kill. The animals appeared in a trance at the sound of Leonard Cohen's voice. Carlos was temporarily calmed, but was unsure of what to do in the longer term. If this happened again, one of them could get killed.

Carlos bought a large print of Leonardo da Vinci's Lady with an Ermine from the Met gift shop. It was his first time leaving the apartment in several days. His black hair was slick with grease, his jeans were ripped, and his jacket smelled of expired leather treatment. A tourist offered him money when he walked through Central Park. Several sections of the park were closed due to flooding, and he inadvertently stomped through a partially flooded area and got his jeans and boots soaked with murky water. When he got the print home, it was wet around the edges. No rain had fallen.

The animals were enamored with the Lady with an Ermine print, except O'Leary, who was indifferent. With the combination of the music and the image, Carlos felt he had gotten them under control, at least for the time being.

He walked to the liquor store and bought a case of wine, six whites and six reds, the first bottles on the entrance's display table. The wine cost $12.99 per bottle, and he walked the box home, despite the pain in his shoulder. He knew that he wasn't responsible for the planning, which included refreshments, but he wouldn't feel right about not providing anything. When he got home, he dropped the box on his small circular kitchen table and heard one of the bottles break. Red liquid bled through the cardboard and leaked onto the black and white tile floor. He sat in his one kitchen chair and watched the pool grow. He cleaned it up later, when it was dark out and the street lamp outside his building flickered.

On Saturday people began arriving shortly after nine. Most faces were unfamiliar. Komiko, Xuan, and Archie had shown up hours earlier to prepare. They were surprised by the lack of furniture, despite having been warned by John Dash Irwin that the place would be mostly bare. The kitchen table would have to act as the main bar. Xuan thundered around the apartment looking for anything on which to place bottles and glassware. She said "What about in here?" pointing to the closed den, and Carlos told her there was nothing in there. She asked if she could check anyway, and he told her that the room was off-limits because it had recently been fumigated. They had brought eight paintings and hung them on the bare walls in the main room. Prices varied from $10,000 to over a million. Once guests began arriving, Komiko acted as a greeter. She and Archie handed out glasses of champagne and tequila sodas, the bottles for which they kept on the rickety wooden floor beside them. Several bottles were knocked over as the place filled. Carlos wore a bomber jacket, jeans, and a baseball cap; he spoke with people he didn't know, most of whom didn't know whose apartment they were in. Carlos failed to understand what this party had to do with him, or how or why his father would care. Komiko had her boyfriend bring over speakers, into which they plugged a laptop, and then the music boomed. "Hey man, what's the wifi password?" "Oh, I don't have one." "What?" "Sorry." John Dash arrived just before eleven. He brought several people with him, including Jennifer Garner, who had cut her hair very short. John Dash was the tallest person in the room, as usual, and his thundering voice still carried despite the noise. Carlos sipped a club soda and nodded at him. "Is there a bird in here?" John Dash sliced through the crowd, parting the bodies with his slender but powerful limbs, his crew tailing him. He wore a multicolored jacket, mostly white, blue, red, and black, which took Carlos a minute to realize was based on Basquiat's Defacement. He could make out the cop swinging the baton. "You look like you're on your way to a peep show," John Dash said to Carlos. "Meet my new friends. This is Frag, Oz, Jennifer, Jackson, Li, and this is Kolorov. He's only 15 so do not let him consume alcohol. He's a chess master. His parents will skin me alive if they find out he took any pollutants." "Hi, nice to meet you all, thanks for coming." Carlos shook everyone's hands and looked at the small boy with the bowl cut called Kolorov. He was an incredibly awkward looking child, with an Angus Young schoolboy outfit and bright red shoes reminiscent of Dorothy's in The Wizard of Oz. "I already took mushrooms," Kolorov said. "Very funny. Cool it with that talk," John Dash said. "Will you buy me a painting?" Kolorov said to Jennifer Garner. "I like that one." He pointed at the oil painting of a grizzly bear sleeping on the desk in an office cubicle at night, with the surrounding buildings visible in the outer dark, scattered lights on in the background. Carlos hadn't paid attention to it until now. "We'll see, sweetie. Carlos, may I ask you a question?" "Sure." "Why don't you have any furniture?" "Well, I..." "He's been systematically decluttering for years, but she's right, this is extreme. This is far beyond minimalism. He'll only be happy once everything is gone. Why do you keep looking over there? What are you sleuthing, Cal?" John Dash said. "Nothing," Carlos said, as he watched three women in white scrutinize the hand-written "Do Not Enter!" sign on the den door. "I really did take mushrooms, Johnny cakes." "Be quiet, you little shit, I do not want or need my buzz hijacked. I have enough trouble as it is." "I know it's loud in here, but did somebody hear something, like, growl?" "Did you call him Cal earlier? Is that your nickname?" "His parents wanted to name him Cal Rose, like Rose as a middle name, but the doc who wrote the birth certificate took too many barbiturates and screwed up the paperwork," John Dash said. Azalea showed up sometime around midnight. "You're such a shit bastard, you invite all these maniacs into your place but you never call me? Ridiculous." "I didn't invite them. This wasn't even my idea." "You're such a bad liar it's remarkably...

Who is that, didn't I see him on The Morning Show?" She did cocaine off her hand. She offered Carlos a bump but he declined. "Sorry, I'd use the washroom, but there's an hour-long line, and I don't think anyone in here gives a damn. I've had a very rough month, thank you for asking. My mother is in the hospital again. They finally diagnosed her with diverticulitis. She'd literally been suffering for years and they just told her to lose weight. This new doctor was like 'holy shit, you could have died! You should sue for malpractice!' But now she's getting treated at least. But they had to remove like a lot of her intestine." "I'm sorry to hear that." People pushed through the crowd, and Carlos got separated from those he knew. "What on earth is that smell?" "Can somebody please, PLEASE help me find my purse?" "I insisted that I would not visit Machu Picchu without eating at Central first, so we got off the plane and cabbed right to the restaurant. They don't have Uber yet. She got Montezuma's revenge the next day so I was spared that horrendous hike anyway. Flawless victory. I need to look at old rubble like I need a bullet in my ass." "Montezuma was Peruvian?" "The fact that The Caretaker's discography isn't on Apple Music or Spotify is the worst thing about modern culture." "Have you guys seen these floods in the Park? It's actually getting really bad. Does anyone even know where the water is coming from?" "You ever heard that old urban legend about the alligator that comes through the sewer system and up through the toilet?" "What year was this place even built?" "1912." "What do you call a Columbia MFA with a prosthetic leg and 100K in student debt?" "Where in the hell is Kolorov? That little bastard better not pull any shit, I need to get him back to his parents in one piece." "Somebody bought the Jimmerson painting! Fuck, I wanted that." "Do you know anyone here with molly or sleeping pills? I can trade Prozac or Adderall but I don't have any cash and I am 100% desperate but I'm not sucking anyone off this time, I cannot deal with these tiles and rando-dick at the same time. It's one or the other." "I am depressed but at this very moment I feel okay so I think that's a win." "Excuse me a moment." Carlos applied new scotch tape to the sign on the den door, which had practically fallen off. He put his ear to the door, but it was hard to hear with all the music and noise. "Stop being weird. How's your sister?" Azalea said. "I haven't spoken to her in a while." Someone bumped into Azalea and she spilled her wine on Carlos. "Watch it, fuck face! Shit, I think that was one of Bloomberg's grandkids. Sorry! Ugh, I got it all over you." "It's okay." "This wine is disgusting anyway, good god. Who are these party planners you hired? Demand a refund." "I didn't hire them." "I think you could seriously get like at least 50% back." "I bought the wine." "You? Ha, I'm sure. Mr. 'If they don't have a Puligny-Montrachet I'm taking a yearlong vow of silence'? Please. Who can I get more drugs from here? Seriously why are you fitzing around with the door? Join the party!" "Where is my bracelet? I got that in Tunis." "What a fight. He tore his bicep in the first round and still fought the full twelve. We were third row center. I got a bunch of his blood on me. Candy pretended to lick it off but she accidentally actually licked it! I posted it in my story. She was mortified." "Okay, seriously, has anyone seen Kolorov? I can't find him," John Dash said, in the kitchen. Carlos shrugged. Jennifer Garner shrugged. "He said he wanted to mingle." "Ugh. He probably got bored and went to get pizza at Iggy's. I'll have to go recover him from Washington Square Park, hustling the chess crazies. This is the third time he's spoiled my evening. Whatever. He can wait." "Why are you babysitting this chess prodigy?" Carlos asked. "It's a long story. And he was a prodigy seven years ago." People came and went throughout the night. Guests started to mostly filter out at around three in the morning. A handful hung around in the kitchen for a while. Carlos and Komiko spoke about art until the sun peeked through the window and the flickering street lamp turned off.

Once everyone was gone, Carlos went into the den. Mojito was chirping and shrieking, trying to pick at Henry's clasped jaw. She had plucked out many of her feathers and looked almost bald on her right side. Mya also had done a number on herself, her front paw slick with blood and saliva from excessive cleaning. She had a somber face. Henry did not look well. He lay in his pool, without the usual smile. He looked bloated and exhausted. Beside the pool, something bright and red attracted Carlos' attention. It was a shoe, just like Dorothy's from The Wizard of Oz. Carlos held it up to the light. It was fairly small in size. O'Leary slept.

The animals were in a bad way. The wound on Mya's paw had become infected. It smelled foul, and she was sickly. Henry seemed worse, as if he'd eaten something that had poisoned him or at least given him serious indigestion. He made deep growls that sounded like the whirring of a truck engine just before stalling. Mojito continued to shriek and pluck out her feathers. "What should I do?" Carlos asked O'Leary. He wanted to call the vet, but was worried they would report the animals for being kept improperly in a residence, and he would be forced to give them up. Henry seemed in dire straits. The contents of his belly might have needed examining.

On Monday the phone rang and Carlos answered in the kitchen after two rings.

"This is the police."

"Oh?"

"We're calling about a missing person that was reportedly at your residence."

"Oh?"

"Kelvin Kolorov, Aged 15. You had a party, as far as we understand? And this young man was a guest, is that correct?"

"I'm really not sure. There were a lot of people here that I didn't know." O'Leary came into the kitchen. Carlos must have left the den door open.

"We have it that mister Kolorov was at your residence from individuals that were with him that night at said residence. They said they introduced you? We're just trying to make heads and tails out of the details, sir. You're not in any trouble."

O'Leary stared at Carlos. He chewed eucalyptus. He ground it to mulch.

"Oh, well yes, maybe. I remember vaguely. I had been drinking, it's all a little blurry."

O'Leary stared at Carlos. He stopped chewing.

"Alright. We're not too worried, to be honest. Probably just with friends. Basement, video games, pizza. We may come by the apartment in the next couple of days, to ask some follow-up questions, should mister Kolorov remain missing."

"Okay."

Carlos spent the next day with the animals; their conditions had not improved. He tried feeding them, butnone wanted to eat.

John Dash Irwin called, colossally drunk, and sobbed as he spoke. "He's missing, Cal, he's missing. Missing! He's gone. He was in my care and now he's gone. Like the fucking wind. His parents, they're connected. High circles. We must find him. You're smart. You know things. Help me please! Don't let me fall. I can't suffer a fall. I don't have any left in me."

He spent all his waking moments with the animals. Were they convalescing or worsening? If they died, what would it matter if they got sent away or not? He rubbed Henry's back. He had the phone in his other hand. Mojito had flown the coop again. He hoped she'd return again but how could he know? He weighed his options, over and over.

I Am Cometh

I sometimes tell people, mainly Marissa, that things feel better in memories. I know that David goes down on me how frat boys do it, like he has nothing to prove and somewhere to be, but he still makes it clear he thinks he's the best at it. His little so-called tricks don't do much other than tickle me. But the memory of it, is nicer, I think, than the reality. I sit in the den, remembering the last time, a few days ago, when it was stormy and the building swayed. After twelve or so minutes he rose, flexing, victorious. He unzipped his pants, and I tied my hair back.

When Alessandro does it, he doesn't have tricks. He's elegant, and it's pleasant. But I'm still somewhere else.

This morning David tried to sleep with me, but I said no. It was my first time rejecting an advance from him since we've all been here. He took it well enough. I moved his hand off my thigh and shook my head. He gulped his beer and said, "Alright," and disappeared somewhere, probably in search of Kayla.

In the afternoon, I'm still in the den, drinking a funky orange wine that Oliver had Simms fetch from the tunnels three weeks ago. I didn't know this sort of thing was available down there and I was happy to discover that it was, even if it wasn't a perfect fit. I'm happy with whatever, honestly. We drink orange wine in the orange afternoon, hundreds of feet above the row, the Park. The weather is starting to turn cold. Other than the balconies, I haven't been outside, like properly outside, in months.

Time feels lost. I'm not sure what day it is. I get dizzy easily, but I lounge on the couch like a Victorian. Marissa leads Alessandro into the den, reacting to my presence, as if they didn't know I had been here, but I'd spent the better part of the last three days in here, mostly with David and a bottle of Belvedere, so I think they knew. My mood might seem different to them because I had a lot of wine. They are on MDMA, some cooked-up version of it from the tunnels, and Alessandro hasn't worn a shirt for a week. He says he is very warm but he has goosebumps. His nipples and abs are hard. He has a body like a ballet dancer.

Marissa licks my neck. I am into it. Alessandro lies there and I sit on him with my tights still on, onto his stubbly jaw, and he licks me through the fabric. I cum with Marissa sucking my nipples, but it doesn't feel as good as I'd hoped. Parts feel numb, inside and out. Alessandro rifles through the black box and finds some things he likes. He asks me to peg him, but I am just too tired, and I say no. Marissa does the honors. He climaxes laughing and screaming with what I think is joy.

Later, only half of us inhabit the double long grey sofa

at dinner like we are alleycats defending our territories. We eat bread, camembert, rosemary manchego, jamon Iberico, some cheese with truffle in it from central Italy, assorted roasted nuts, and cans of seafood like scallops and octopuses, all collected by Simms in the tunnels over the week. The foie gras is a very nice surprise; I had forgotten about it. The wooden plank we all eat from, carried out from the west kitchen by David and Moyo, came from a tree Daddy cut down himself, from our old cottage, when I was a kid. The tree was named Elcie. I gave it that name, but I don't remember when. Simms fills our glasses with sparkly golden wine as we eat. He has finally stopped wearing his bowtie. Some watch the rerun of reality TV on the massive screen, others look outside watching the other 57th Street towers that sway with us. Andrea sits on the couch with her legs over my shoulders, massaging my head. She never eats anything anymore.

*

The window in the great room stretches twenty feet across and touches the ceiling, a portal to the sky. If you look down at Central Park, you can see the flooding clearly, even from this high. The Park has become a swamp. It's like looking at a map placed over a coffee stain, and watching the moisture bleed through the paper. The rumor, from the tunnels, is a crocodile now roams the moats and cesspools of The Park, spitting out human bones.

"How would it have gotten to Manhattan?" David asks of Simms.

"The zoo, perhaps?" Simms offers.

David snorts. "Yeah, obviously. It was rhetorical."

Simms always greets me in the morning by taking a tiny bow, as he says, "Miss Rose." He's so tall I feel like a baby when he passes, which is funny because he's been with our family since I was a baby, so I wonder how I felt looking up at him back then. He's very nice and polite and I feel safe with him here, even when Daddy is gone.

If you stand at the window at the right moment, the orange evening light gets so bright that it wraps around your whole body. Even facing north, sunbeams reflect off shorter buildings from east and west and meet on your face.

I stand in it and picture myself inside a fire. I close my eyes. A hand reaches across my body.

I imagine the old cottage. My earliest memory is picking raspberries off the vines and eating them. My hands stained red. Convinced in a dream panic that it was blood. The taste of the raspberries kept me from crying. The cottage was small. Mom's idea. She liked simple things. My brother Carlos liked it too. Daddy would never go for something so modest now.

The hand pulls me backwards, into a body. Another hand is in front of my mouth. I open wide.

A pill is put on my tongue. I swallow it.

Through my eyelids I can feel burning. I see the color. I hear oceans, waterfalls, fire raging, a house collapsing.

*

My best friend was Hannah but she died from the

floods, when they first came. Maybe it's good she isn't here. She wouldn't approve. I got sad thinking about her yesterday. She got her driver's license before me. When Daddy would go out of town, we would steal his Maserati and she'd screech through the streets at three in the morning so fast that I would get sick and vomit on my shoes, my white Keds that I bought in a grocery store in Queens. They cost six dollars. She'd drive so fast that cops would put their lights on and she would try to outrun them, and was successful twice before they got her. Her dad taught her how to drive. He was a mechanic who worked on race cars. She was a tomboy and hated when guys would hit on her or make fun of her. She broke Trevor Stollighurst's nose when he called her "surfboard" after grabbing her ass, and nobody said anything rude to her after that. Trevor's parents wanted to press charges but he stopped them because he was embarrassed. They actually became friends after. She tried to drop out because she hated school but her parents told her she'd be cut off if she did. We got our nipples pierced together on her 18th birthday. The anniversary is a week from now. I wish I could be in the car with her again, a lit cigarette in her mouth, smoky tears in our eyes, doing 140 on Broadway. Now there's no more cars. Not in this borough. Not anywhere near here.

*

Ferran has been carrying Daddy's shotgun for the last two days. He raided the walk-in closet looking for suits. He took Ketamine and spent six hours trying on every piece of clothing, as if they'd fit differently. Daddy's at least six inches taller than Ferran. He eventually came out wearing a navy three-piece with a red tie, subtle paisley in the fabric (yuk, it's one of Daddy's ugliest), with the matte black 12-gauge draped across his shoulder as if he was the world's coolest killer guy. He was wearing his sunglasses too, Daddy's sunglasses. This obviously wouldn't fly if Daddy were here, but he's been gone for a year, and I don't know when he's coming back. There are no flights leaving The UAE and that's an indefinite thing. I know he must be worried about me. At least he knows I'm with friends.

Ferran stopped eating four days ago. He looks really ripped with a shirt off but insists that he must lose five or six more percent of body fat before he'll eat again. He drinks water and champagne and coffee, but that's it. Marissa said she saw him eat a hard-boiled egg the other night, that he had Simms wake up and boil him one solitary egg and Simms didn't question it. He put on his whole suit just to do it, asked Ferran if he wanted salt or pepper, then went back to his room, back to bed. I don't like people going into Simm's room and asking him for things, especially when he's sleeping. It's one of my few rules but Ferran still broke it.

Ferran sits with the shotgun in his lap at all times. Sometimes he cradles it like an infant or a cat. He is self-conscious about his height. He took scissors and cut the bottoms of Daddy's pants. Normally I would have freaked out but I just said, "That looks silly," and left it at that. He is swimming in the jacket. He holds the shotgun close to him like it's a sweet child. He won't go anywhere in the condo without it.

Andrea seemed keen at first but soon made it obvious that she didn't like it here. She never said that in any kind of explicit way, but she just wasn't herself after she got here. Some people said she hadn't been right since the floods started. Maybe it was before that. She'd sit on the top of the couch in the library and stare at nothing for hours. She'd stare at you if you came into the room, and if you tried to talk to her, she'd turn away and face another direction. She kept her tied hair back, which she normally never did. She always used to wear it down, perfectly straightened. She has the most amazing beautiful straight hair. Everyone is jealous of and intimidated by her. She's six feet tall and walks with such grace and confidence that if she were coming toward you on the street you'd jump out of the way. But since she's been here, we've all been worried. You could sit down and watch TV in the library room and she wouldn't care. She'd sometimes wander over to the other couch, the leopard print, which was not preferred because there was a rip in the leather from David on the first night. He did too many drugs and cut the couch open pretending to do an autopsy on an ancient dead god he'd unearthed.

David was the one who moved a TV into the library room because he said it had the most comfortable couches in the whole penthouse, and that it was the perfect spot to watch sports, but there wasn't much to watch, hardly anything in the way of live sports or new shows. Daddy would absolutely not approve, but he's not here and I'm sick of fighting with David and Ferran about their little habits so I just let it be.

Before all this, Andrea had the reputation for being the sex queen of the Lower East Side. She was discerning, but devastating. She made a few rich young men lose their minds. They'd stalk her and weep outside her building all hours of the night, back when she could still access her building. Security would escort these guys away like they were homeless, crazy, like they were nuisances, mosquitos. One of them was heir to a plastics fortune with his own boutique airline. He spent two nights in a row with Andrea, and when she didn't call him for three days he lost his mind, and last she heard he had a serious drug problem and needed constant clinical help. Who knows now where he is. Probably not in a good place.

No one here has ever had any kind of sexual relation with Andrea. But everyone heard she was coming and I think it's probably why a bunch of them showed up in the first place. They thought she'd be like a piece of meat or something. Kayla has been asking her for advice, about how to do all kinds of things, and Andrea has given her one-word answers. I feel bad for Kayla because she is clearly homesick and stressed, but I guess so is Andrea. In another world maybe they'd be friends. Or maybe Andrea would be a mentor to her. Kayla has often said she doesn't have a positive role model in her life.

He won't say anything, not yet at least, but I can tell David is pissed that Andrea isn't putting out. He expected free love, no questions asked. In fairness, that is what I promised. But only from myself. I can't speak for everyone. David looks at Andrea with righteous contempt now. The other night he was drunk and wanted to say something nasty but she looked at him and even in his drunken state he cowered. He was swearing and muttering to himself in the other room. I'm not worried about Andrea, she can handle herself, but she is not happy and I don't feel good about people being in my place unhappy.

Andrea let me brush her hair the other night. Normally she does it to me, which seems to bring her comfort, but she doesn't like people touching her hair, except the other night she changed her mind. She sat at the foot of the couch and I sat above her with her incredible hair splayed out across my legs. I used my mom's old brush, the only one she ever used. I asked Andrea if she was upset because of the floods, if she was worried about the future, and she didn't answer, but I could tell she felt comforted by me, so I just kept brushing. I didn't realize I was doing it at first, whispering, "Shhhh, shhhh, shhhh."

*

I had been texting with my first love Simon up until about six months ago, and I haven't heard from him since. I know he was living in Seattle and had just had a kid and I don't know what's happening there, with the army and the blockades and everything, so I am somewhat worried, but he has his own life now and there's nothing much I can do. The Northwest is its own mess. I don't think Simon would ghost me, but maybe he's just AWOL because having a kid forces you to put everything else on standby at the best of times, and I can only imagine that having a baby at a time like this must be a whole new kind of difficult. I miss Simon very much and really hope I get to see him again one day, and meet his wife and his baby.

I had been dating Gavin when I met Simon. Gavin was the one who Daddy's work partner set me up with, the asset manager who was the son of a stockbroker who was the son of a stockbroker who was the son of a farmer. Those were his words. He loved ending with farmer. We'd been dating three months when Gavin flew us to Las Vegas in a private Gulfstream, and we had champagne in the night, overlooking the dazzle of the strip as we landed. He knew how to treat a girl, but it was all a bit much after a couple days. We played roulette and he lost almost a hundred thousand dollars over a few hours, and I was unbelievably bored, when I wasn't busy wondering what his father would think. The next day I made Gavin rent a car, which made him uncomfortable because he said other people's germs and bad vibes would be all over the seats, even though he had no problem touching Bellagio chips, and he insisted it had to be a Mercedes and I said I didn't like those because Princess Diana died in one, but he said I wasn't even born when she died, and he insisted, in the least charming manner. I knew he wanted to stay in Las Vegas for his own reasons but I wanted to drive far and didn't tell him that at first. We drove through the desert; he said he wanted to turn back after a couple hours, that we didn't know where the gas stations were, out there in the empty red nothingness, among the canyons, that anything could happen, but I said we needed to see more. At a certain point he stopped the car and refused to drive any further, so I said, "Fine, I'll do it." There was some pouty behavior but he couldn't keep it up forever, and I got in the driver's seat, even though I didn't have a license, and I kept driving west. My dear Hannah had taught me how to drive over the years, in fast sports cars, so I knew what I was doing well enough. I don't know why Gavin didn't just turn the car around and drive us back to Vegas. I'll never really know why he gave in. Maybe because he knew who Daddy was and didn't want to upset his daughter. Maybe he was just a baby. We drove through the day and into the night and didn't stop. Gavin slept and I drove. I didn't have any drugs or anything, just coffee and Red Bull from a desert gas station, with an unlit sign, in a barren county, where the kid behind the counter smoked hash-dipped cigarettes as he served us, and had an open wound on his arm, and a tattoo on the other arm that said, "You'll see it all soon." We ended up in San Francisco, where the first thing we did was eat dumplings and drink beer from unmarked white cans in a dirty restaurant with grease stains on the carpet, that was in the back of another restaurant in the Tenderloin district. Our server was big and scary looking, but he was nice to us and didn't mind that we looked like we belonged somewhere else. Gavin had gone silent, while I was chatty and full of light air and having the time of my life. Midway through the meal he got up and said he was going to go suss out hotels. He was gone a while. Our server felt bad for me sitting there alone so he sat with me even though he was busy. He said his name was Simon. His mother was from China and his dad was from Serbia. He said his dad had been a refugee from the Balkan war, who saw his own father shot dead in front of him. He said he'd been in jail before and had had problems with drugs, but was doing better. He had tattoos on his hands and on his legs, and was an expert juggler and had been a piano prodigy when he was younger but now only played when he was bored or couldn't figure something out on his guitar. He brought me extra food, crazy stuff I'd never seen before, and I ate it all, while Gavin was still outside on the phone.

I told Simon that I'd be happy to go with him. I didn't realize I meant it when I said it. Simon blew off work right then and there and we left out the side door and went to his place, where I stayed for three months. We slept together every single day, even for those few days when he had a very bad knee that he said was from falling at work, but was actually from getting in a fight in Lafayette Park, and I had to be on top and be very careful and gentle so as not to hurt him. He introduced me to his crazy friends, like Josep from Paris who lived in San Francisco with no Visa and taught English to African immigrants and sold used car batteries, or Melanie, the exotic dancer with whom Simon had his own secret language that no one else could understand, whose cousin had died of an overdose two days after I met her but she was in great spirits because she said, "death is only the door," and who believed that heroin use was the only true path, and that those who didn't use it were incomplete, as if it was some kind of destiny to succumb to the drug, or Zak who painted vulgar, beautiful murals and was the Bay Area's self-proclaimed most wanted vandal, as none of his work was sanctioned and it was all considered illegal graffiti and terribly obscene, but he was impossible to catch, despite only having one eye, having lost the other one when he was six and his brother shot him with a BB gun, that same brother now an optometrist, or Angel, who had seven children, all boys, all with different fathers, four of whom were dead or missing, who was by far the nicest human being I'd ever met, who had to drink her coffee cold because of the damage done to her throat from the pipe, who's hair touched the floor and who's voice sounded like the stars. We would run all over the city, sneaking onto streetcars with no coins, hopping out of cabs without paying, ditching bills in restaurants, smoking cigarettes in movie theatres, security guards with flashlights looking for us as we made quick exits. Normally I could have paid for all these things without even thinking about it, but Daddy had cancelled my credit cards by then. I still pictured Gavin out there on the phone, outside the restaurant, where I left him. It was the last time I saw him. I imagined him out there, waiting for me. I wondered how he went back to New York. Did he fly back from San Fran or did he drive the rented Mercedes back to Las Vegas first? Simon told me he was sober, but he meant just from drugs because we drank together all the time. But I would see him smoke joints, which he said didn't count. Then I saw him arranging a needle and spoon in a drawer once and I knew but I didn't say anything. A few days after he asked me if I wanted to try and I shook my head. He didn't pressure me, but he went into the bathroom and didn't come out, and I had to go in and collect him, asleep on the toilet, and put him to bed. I loved him very much and wanted him to be happy. After Daddy sent Conrad and Mick to come find me, it took me a very long time to forgive him. I don't know how they found me, but that's Daddy for you. Conrad knocked on the door and

I opened it without checking even though Simon had a needle in his arm, and they came in and grabbed me and I knew it was all over. I didn't make a sound, I just cried silently, until Simon looked up and smiled and Conrad hit him in the face, and then kicked him on the ground when he saw the needle, that was when I screamed.

Years later, Simon told me that he was sober for real. I heard honesty in his voice and I made the decision to believe him. Only then did I forgive Daddy. Maybe he didn't deserve forgiveness, but I am not vindictive. I think about San Francisco now, about how the floods are affecting it probably worse than here. About Simon. I was overjoyed when he told me he had a child, it was a true miracle. His wife is a nurse. He hasn't responded to my texts for months. I hope he is okay, he and his family. I hope they are in a place of peace. But I can't know.

*

Alessandro stands at the window every morning, the first one awake, usually naked, watching the floods. He doesn't say anything, just watches the stable water line, impossible to really gauge it in a meaningful way from this high. Marissa is behind him and clutches his chest. They stand together, looking down. They do drugs together every day, but they don't have so much sex anymore. The glee on their faces, even when high, seems less pronounced now, more of a mask to hide the fear and the uncertainty. Kayla tells them not to worry. They say they're not. David laughs, at them, at something in his head. He takes off his clothes, asks who wants to go. People ignore him, but eventually him and Kayla go behind a closed door. Simms serves breakfast and goes to the elevator. He has bags under his eyes. I think to myself he should retire but that seems far-fetched now. Retirement happens in comfortable circumstances. Simms's job, feeding us and keeping us healthy and stable enough to go on, for now, in a time like this, as uncertain as we all are, is not a job that one retires from.

*

I sit with Moyo in the library. He tells me that he is afraid for the future, in his soft, delicate voice. We hold hands but it's not romantic, just comforting. Moyo is the tallest person here, even taller than Simms, and in many ways the most beautiful, but I haven't seen him engage in any kind of sex with anyone. He had a boyfriend before the floods, Arnold, still has I suppose, but doesn't know where he is now. I tell Moyo he has nothing to worry about, that as long as we are here, everything is safe. We have everything we need. Moyo says he's worried about Arnold and his parents, who he assumes all live in the tunnels, and must be suffering. Moyo was in the art gallery, literally at a gallery opening featuring his own work, when the news of the floods began. Andrea brought him here, the last to join us. We knew what was coming, but we didn't know how suddenly it would devastate everything. I can only imagine how people in the tunnels are living. I pray for those people. Moyo hadn't seen his parents for years before the floods because they'd kicked him out of the house long ago, but Moyo still loves them. Moyo tells me that his parents are self-sufficient and will eat rats in the tunnels to survive if they need to, but Arnold isn't. I assure him that that's probably not necessary, that the tunnels are flush with vendors and food, however basic, and people are probably doing okay there. In truth I don't really know. I tell Moyo I'm very happy I know him. One day we will see his work in galleries all over the world, when we've solved all of this. I tell Moyo he is in good hands. We hold each other for a long time, into the night, and fall asleep together. I wake up in the middle of the night. It's black and silent. Moyo's arms are around me, the arms of a guardian angel, and I feel the comfort around me like a blanket. I lie awake until the sun comes up, painting the room orange.

*

Simms spends a concerning amount of time down in the tunnels today. Normally he is gone for two to three hours at a time. But today he leaves early, around seven in the morning. He doesn't come back in his usual timely fashion. By noon, no one appears to notice or care, but I do. He is usually efficient. By mid-afternoon, as I'm getting worried, pacing, things get worse because Marissa informs me that Andrea has left. I play dumb and ask her, "What do you mean, left?" but I already know. This place is not for her. I tell myself she went down there to look for Simms but I know that's not true. She just left. I don't know for sure, but I fear I may never see her again.

It's nearly six in the evening when I hear the ding

of the elevator and breathe a sigh of relief to see Simms slope out. He walks with a limp that he doesn't hide well, carrying his usual bag of procurements. I ask no questions, I just give him a nod.

"Miss Rose."

He drops the bags on the kitchen table without emptying them and goes to his room. David is shirtless in the kitchen, eating a pear and a tin of Galician octopus. He says, "Job's not done, Jeeves!" and follows Simms to his room. I follow after David because this is inappropriate and Daddy would not want anyone going into Simms's room except me.

Simms takes off his jacket as I burst in after David. Simms's white shirt is soaked red.

"Is that blood?" David says. "Jesus, shit."

"It's quite alright, it's just a shirt. It looks worse than it is. I'll be fine. Please don't concern yourself." Simms lies down on the bed without taking off the shirt, and stains the sheets beneath him streaky red.

"Okay. Okay. He wants to be alone," David says. He looks nervous, panicked. "We should respect that. Come on."

I turn around to leave, to give Simms privacy, as David grabs me by the arm and leads me out. I pull my arm away from him.

"Are you nuts? Look at him," I say.

"I'm fine," Simms says. "I'll prepare dinner shortly."

"He says he's fine," David says.

I push David aside and lift Simms off the bed by the arm, cradling it around my neck. I've never lifted anything this heavy before and it takes a great deal of strain but something has taken over me. Simms is skinny but very tall, so it is not only heavy but awkward.

"Can I have some help, please?"

David grabs Simms' other arm, and the burden on my neck eases.

"Unhand me," Simms says.

"No way, tough guy. You need attention," David says.

We help him to the bathroom. Simms doesn't fight, as we walk together, clambering through the hall, one shaky step at a time. I take Simms's shirt off, revealing a body so emaciated and spotty it looks like it's not real. I don't see bodies that look like this. He has a small but very deep wound on his side.

"What happened?" I say.

"Bit of a disagreement is all," Simms says.

"Now we're bros," David says, pointing at his own body, a scar he has on his side, which as far as I know he got tripping onto barbed wire while drunk.

"The water!" I say.

David runs the bath and I help Simms get all his clothes off, even his underwear, and then we get him into the tub. David doesn't make any crude jokes, to my surprise. He holds a towel against Simms' side, and I go get the tape.

I run into Daddy's office, the smaller one on this floor, and scour the desk for tape, but find nothing of the sort.

I run back across the floor and Alessandro is in the hallway eating a piece of cheese with headphones in and says, "What happened?"

I go into the kitchen and remember the first aid kit under the sink. I bring the whole thing back into the bathroom and hand it to David. He looks through it until he finds a special kind of gauze. Simms takes the towel away and David holds him up as I apply the gauze carefully. I wrap it around Simms's torso.

"This'll feel tight as virgin ass, but don't shimmy. Just try to be still and let it do its thing. This stuff is the best option other than stitches, at least for now," David says, like he knows things.

"Alright," Simms says.

I have my phone in my hand and I text Simon even though I know I won't get an answer. I text him that I miss him and hope his wife and child are doing well and hope I can see him again soon.

David says he stitched himself up once when he kicked a window while drunk, and thinks he could stitch Simms if he had a needle and thread, but the stab wound looks deep and doesn't know if it's hit any vital things, and that Simms probably needs medical attention. He says he has a friend, a doctor, that's in the tunnels, but doesn't know what his situation is. He texts his doctor friend. We will have to wait and see.

We eventually carry Simms to his bed, after he is dry. He is awake but exhausted. We give him orange juice, and soup which Marissa heats from a can.

David's doctor friend doesn't respond.

*

"Do I fear for the future? Hell fucking no I don't. Hell no. You know why? Because fear is dumb wasted pussy shit that serves no purpose. That's why. We'll figure this out like we figure everything. Pass that over. Should we start a cult? Who said that? They probably have two dozen cults down there and they probably already have it nailed, down pat, down rat, systems established, whole nine yards, established, organized. Probably two million cults. We couldn't do a cult cause there's only a handful of us up here and like the whole point is you need to convince other people, people who aren't part of your crew, susceptible people, stupid people, plebs, and we are not that, and also the girls are too rational except Kayla, you'd fall for shit easy, like slipping on banana peels, don't deny it, haha. Ow! That shit hurts! She may look weak but she punches like a guy. You know why I don't fear the future is cause I've seen the future I've pictured it I've imagined it, it looks way worse than this or whatever else. I've seen a giant black walking tower of black bile and limbs and filth like the size of One World Trade or like a mountain but like with legs, dripping black blood and shit, swinging its thousand-foot dick which happens to have an axe where the head should be, a swinging pendulum of death that cums lava, saying in the deepest, vilest, most ear-shattering voice 'I AM COMETH! I AM COMETH!' as it pisses black sludge down on entire cities, vile dark liquid that melts buildings, and when people hear its voice they instantly die of terror. Everything becomes dust. This thing wipes out cities, countries, continents, entire armies can't take it down, even with fighter jets and nukes. That's what's coming. One day. Eventually, let me tell you, so no, for god's sake I don't fear the future, I know this is all a dream, I know this is what we make it. Pass me that! Why, do you fear for the future? You know what,

I don't want to know."

*

It takes David a while to wake but eventually he gets up and he and I go to Simms's room. His doctor friend did not respond. Simms hasn't left the bed, hasn't gotten up. He is perfectly still. David checks his pulse and puckers his lips, looks at me. He checks again. He puts his head down. He reaches for his phone. He looks like he wants to text someone but he doesn't.

"I guess you have to tell your dad," David says, and walks out of the room.

It smells musky in here. Not just foul exactly, but unclean.

David is quiet the rest of the day. Moyo and Marissa spend hours with him in the den, drinking. I join them here and there, but mostly I am by myself. I spend some time with Alessandro. There's a tone of silent mourning throughout the house.

At some point Alessandro says, "What do we do with the body?"

It's not clear to me if he's asking how we properly dispose of the body, or if he is asking, or maybe suggesting, whether or not we will in fact get rid of the body, like maybe he means we might want to keep it. In case we run out of food, or as a memento, something like that. I don't know the answer.

I still haven't texted Daddy.

I stare at the closed elevator door.

Alessandro once told me he used to eat sandwich

crusts out of garbage bins at school, because his parents never had enough money to send him to school with full meals. If I think that everyone here would be opposed to eating some less than perfectly desirable meals, I am probably wrong. Maybe I'm not wrong. I don't know.

*

David is a drunk, sloppy mess. He goes into Simms' room and tries to pour whiskey into his mouth, and Moyo has to wrestle him out. Moyo whispers to David, trying to calm him down, but it only works temporarily. David hangs out by the window, playing a game with Ferran, who is also out of his mind. Still obsessed with Daddy's shotgun, Ferran marches like a soldier, wearing no clothes, holding only the shotgun, answering any question at the top of his lungs, "Yes, sir!" "No, sir!", pronouncing the word sir as if it had an A in it, like "Yes sar!" He never sits, spends all day standing by windows, as if he's keeping watch, as if David's rants last night scared the reason out of him, and he now waits with Daddy's weapon.

David asks Ferran questions, like "Are you the product of a squirrel and a pine cone?" "Did you have Fruit Loops as a child in Spain?" "Are you hiding from us the meaning of life?" all of which Ferran answers with increasingly loud "No sars!" David asks Ferran if he thinks he can kick through the window in the great room, and Ferran says "Yes sar!" and David says to prove it, and I say as nicely as I can that I don't think that's a good idea, and David says prove it, and I say it's against Daddy's rules, no kicking windows. Ferran seems to understand the concept

136

of rules, because he does nothing, which pisses David off, and he kicks at the window with the heel of his foot, once, twice, and on the third try his whole legs goes through the glass.

The sound of the glass breaking is like a thud. David falls onto the ground, his naked leg sticking into the Manhattan air, caught in an orbit of stabbing shards. He is laughing, but I see the pain on his face. Moyo is standing, braced, not sure what to do. Kayla hides her face in her hands, repeating "Oh my god!" Marissa says, "Do something!" which Ferran interprets to mean him, so he does his duty and blasts out the window with a round from Daddy's gun. Everyone ducks. My ears ring so loudly that I can't hear anything. David pulls himself back into the apartment, shaking, terrified, the sky blowing into our home, cooling us, delivering us the evening air, that fresh beautiful air, mixing with glass and dust. David's blood spreads across the floor. I am not angry. Moyo brings towels and presses them to David's leg. Marissa looks like she's going to say something, but I tell her where the first aid kit is. Ferran has a little burn on his chest, where the shell bounced back. He puts his hand to it, and looks up at the sky, like he's done good in the world.

Later, when I go to see David while he lies in bed, leg bandaged, blood still soaking through, he tells me he's sorry he couldn't help Simms. He says he did his best. I tell him it's okay. He repeats that he did his best. He continues to echo himself. I hold his hand and tell him it's okay. He asks me if I've lost people. I remind him about my mother. I don't think he understands what he's saying. He's been through a lot.

He asks me if I fear for the future. I tell him I don't.

*

I see an angel rise above us this morning. I look out the window and there she is. She is twelve feet tall, with hair that tumbles below her feet, and feathered wings big enough for a jumbo jet. I am not scared. She floats in front of me with closed eyes, and I close mine as well, with my hands on the glass, and I feel her.

*

It's cold throughout our great penthouse. The wind continues to scream, louder by the minute, always rising, as it blows in through the broken window. Simms would have known who to contact to fix it, someone down there.

We all eat dinner around the kitchen table. Ferran sits with us and picks at an end piece of bread. David has his leg hoisted on an extra chair, a cushion underneath it. We used antiseptic liquid to clean his gashes, the smell of which made me dizzy, not because it was toxic, but because the smell reminded me of the hospital, when my mother was there, the last time. I remember little about it, but that smell. And Carlos' face. Old enough to understand but too young to understand.

The angel I saw yesterday reminded me of my mother. It's not that she looked like her, but that I felt her presence.

I miss my brother. I worry about him. I should message him, even though he doesn't speak to me very much, and isn't very good with the phone. I worry, with the floods, what Carlos will do, how he will help himself.

I haven't looked at my phone for almost a day, and when I check it this evening, I see I have a text from Simon. Maybe my eyes are making it up. I open it and it's a long text, saying that he's sorry he hasn't gotten back to me in a while, that life has been nonstop chaos, his words exactly, but that he and the baby and his wife are doing fine, that they are navigating the changing days, that he misses me very much, and hopes that all of this will blow over, and I'll be able to visit, that Seattle is doing better now than it was earlier in the year. Something about his text feels dishonest, but I ignore the feeling, as best I can. He doesn't specify what he means by "this." I have to assume, all of this. We all assume, all of this.

A great sensation of relief rolls over me like mountain fog. It's warm and I am sad and happy at the same time. I hold the phone to my body as if it's a tiny little person.

Length

Marguerite won the short story contest. Several famous authors had entered, and she beat them all, and did so with a story of only 100 words. She went to receive her check and her little certificate from the literary magazine's office. The stout editor with the two-colored mustache presented her the award and shook her hand. She felt amazing. Outside she sat on a bench and ate a hotdog and drank Coke from a glass bottle. A tall man with an oily leather jacket sat next to her and asked her about the certificate. I won a literary contest, she said. Did it with only 100 words. The man said Congratulations! Did you know Hemingway once wrote a story that was only six words long? Marguerite nodded as she swallowed her last mouthful of hotdog. She smashed the Coke bottle against the bench and stabbed the man in the liver.

The man survived for three weeks before succumbing to his injury. Marguerite declared her innocence, in court and to her family. She maintained that she broke no law and did no wrong, but she was found guilty, and went to prison.

She never stopped writing, despite incarceration. Over the years she entered countless literary contests. When she was in her forties, she won a contest with a story that was a single word in length. An article was published about the convicted murderer literary genius. An agent came to see her, a hotshot with three Pulitzer winners to his name, and tried to convince her to write a novel. Marguerite refused to speak, and wrote the word NO on a piece of paper in big letters and slid it to the agent. The agent came to see her a few more times, but failed to convince her to write a novel. Marguerite responded with the same one word answer each time. She spent her time writing and thinking, and attending literature classes in prison, which often featured material she was familiar with, but she was happy to be able to have books to read and discuss. The classes were taught by an elderly woman named June, who had lost an eye to cancer and a leg to diabetes, and who was so passionate about books that she would get so worked up discussing class material that she'd run out of breath. Marguerite always worked hard and contributed in class. She took the same course every year, and received the same certificate over and over. She framed each one.

She was sixty when she was released. She took a job at a bookstore, and on her first day she noticed that a book had been written about her life, unbeknownst to her, by the literary agent that came to see her when she was inside. The book began by mentioning that Ernest Hemingway famously wrote a story that was only six words long.

Marguerite closed the book. She sat on a bench on her lunch break, and ate nothing.

Headwalking

June was sick of hearing girls can't mosh, on message boards and in the halls and even from friends like Andrew and Chode, so she set out to prove it wasn't so, first with the mini knife on the wrist that no one noticed, then with the half sleeve, which Beth and Alexa said was a bit much for a former eighth grade gymnastics silver medallist and former Miss Junior Ionia County, then with a full sleeve by the end of the year, complete with blocky Xs on both fists, D.R.U.G on her right knuckles, and F.R.E.G on her left, the G a heinous mistake by Pokey Scholl in his first week at Rug Burn Tattoo and Piercing, the potent cocktail of Adderall and compressed air still dancing in his brain, and despite the error June still vowed never to drink or smoke again, but at the xSurvivorx show she was shoved out and forced to the back of the pit by the boys, almost losing an eye in the process to a spin kick that forced her to spend most of the set in the washroom holding her face with a damp clump of toilet paper, a little bit of blood on her Cold World shirt, doing her own expert makeup for the next two weeks to encourage an unblemished pretence from the eye, Her mother and step-dad not buying it when she swore that she got hit by a falling acorn, dropped from a high branch with vengeance by a deranged squirrel as she sat under her favourite tree in Connaught field, nor did they buy that she wasn't hiding the artwork on her arms and knuckles behind an XXL Bane hoodie she stole from a coat-check years before, and she was in 99% despair mode, ready to run away, sleep on a bench, hitchhike, anything to get away, when she got wind that Knuckle Sandwich were finally playing a show after a five-year hiatus, news that made her and Andrew and Chode beat their heads against their lockers in anticipation, because they remembered that at the last Knuckle Sandwich show six people left in ambulances and Oren Okowski lost his two front teeth, which was why he wore veneers, and which June learned only recently was how he'd earned the nickname Beaver, so she took her time with a mannequin's head she'd stolen from The Levi's Store, drawing convincing blood and gore around the cream neck, adding firm horse hair and painting realistic facial features, and when the show finally came she snuck the head in under her jacket, pretending to be pregnant, which particularly upset Mack Jones who was working the door and hadn't seen June in months and had always had a crush on her, and she bided her time, at the back of the venue, waiting through the openers, avoiding conversation, glassy-eyed, in the zone, until Knuckle Sandwich emerged and opened with Ten Count, her cue to unearth the head from her ruse of a pregnant belly, and ran as fast as she could through the circle, swinging the fiberglass and plastic head by the hair like a Morning Star, mashing anonymous faces, noting Beaver in the crowd scrunching out a panicked Oh Shit! face, and within seconds the crowd cleared, as June swung for her life, and then rushed the stage for the singalong, thrusting the mannequin head up to the mic as Pete Knuckles shoved it at her, and the mannequin head owned the moment, with the crowd behind her carrying the words, security forcing their way through the pit to hoist June and her weapon out of there, everyone screaming, manic, bloodied, June hoisting the head trophy-style, twirling it by the hair like a helicopter blade, screaming the final lyrics to Ten Count, foaming at the mouth, pit queen, if only for a minute

Scorch Earth

An earwig slithers across the black plastic air-conditioning vent. I examine this earwig with intention as Father drives. I at once want and want not to touch it.

I do not like how Father drives the van. I find he is too slow the majority of the time, and then in little unpredictable bursts, too fast. Father is not prone to rage, but behind the wheel he is a different version of himself. Docile, with a chance of acrimony. Not like Mother, who is never calm, even if she appears to be. I would like to examine the earwig closer, but I fear Father will react negatively if I touch it. I wonder if it will survive for long if I leave it to its own devices. Mother would most likely be able to answer that question. I consider whether I should ask her about earwigs when Father and I return home. Even though she is not an entomologist, I am confident that if she refuses an answer, it won't be for lack of expertise but rather out of bewilderment at the question's relevance.

Father takes the turn and smiles as he sees my expression change, because I know we are close to our destination, our favorite Sunday destination. Only eight to ten more minutes, depending on traffic. There is rarely any traffic here, this far outside Denver. But I have calculated that, because of the occasional tourist convoy, as people do sometimes venture here to get their views of the Rockies, there should be at least a one-minute-average differential, just in case. But this is early in the season, and the likelihood is that we are eight minutes away.

He leans over and kisses my head and says, "Almost there, sweetheart," which he does at exactly this point every Sunday.

*

I am a god of war

*

My desk is four feet high with only one and a half feet of depth to the wall. It is completely white. Whenever Yuliana comes over and attempts to sit at my desk she launches the same complaint every time, that the desk is far too small to fit any kind of computer or homework or anything else of any significance, and that there is virtually no legroom available as the desk sits against the wall. I find my desk perfectly adequate for my needs. I am not large. My laptop screen is only thirteen inches across.

At the moment I am listening to two separate podcasts. My English homework is open on my desk but I am procrastinating. Mother says procrastination is unacceptable. But she and Father are discussing something downstairs that I have ranked a seven out of ten on the hostility scale. It will be at least thirty minutes before there is silence. My door is closed. I cannot hear the details about the argument, but I can discern from the tone, it's a seven out of ten.

I am drinking water from my favorite porcelain tea mug. I drink tea out of it as well, but not after 5:00 P.M. Mother does not approve of caffeine so late. I prefer the cup to all other vessels because it is ornate and makes me feel as if I am a member of a forgotten royal family, not the princess or the heiress to a throne, but rather some kind of niece who lives in the palace and to whom no one speaks because all of the proper pretty girls are terrified of her, so they leave her to her own devices, whereby she spends her days reading books of ancient mysticism, books about anatomy, books about weaponry, and, with great diligence, books about killing. The cup is white, as is its saucer. Both are adorned with a series of oceanic blue waves of such detail that they can induce a spell of hypnosis should they be gazed upon for too long. After a few servings of tea, one becomes used to the cup's artistry, but I still find myself taken by it.

There is only one other object in the house that I cherish equally.

The two podcasts are on simultaneously, one headphone in each ear. One, about the current state of the climate on planet Earth, is playing from my computer. It is a conversation between two men and a woman. One man is the host, the other is someone who wrote a book. The woman is a professor. They seem to agree that the Earth is in peril, but there is a general tone of argumentativeness about them, possibly because the subject matter scares them and the prospect of annihilation reduces them to angry, irrational animals. The other podcast, which is playing from my phone, is about living a purpose-driven life. There is a single woman speaking. I am paying more attention to her words than those of the speakers in the other podcast, but I am able to listen to both. Her words are mostly derived from a book that she didn't write, and though I only found this podcast because she and I share the same first name, Lily, I am generally interested in the subject matter. A purpose-driven life. It is a topic of much discussion in this house. Perhaps Mother would even approve.

*

I am an angel of death

*

I am observing the earwig when Father makes the turn. The trees disappear and in front of us is a long road, flanked by flat fields. I love this part of the drive. Only, Father is driving oddly slowly. I am observing the earwig when Father comes to a stop. I don't see another car anywhere. In front of us is a different sort of wreckage. The animal is ripped in half. The smear of blood and gore stretches across dozens of meters of road. I can see the animal's intestines and some other dark organ that looks like a sack of blood. Father gets out of the car without shutting off the engine. I exit as well and we stand over this deer-like creature as if we are at its funeral. Some bones are exposed. A leg is three meters away. Its eyes are still open and it looks calm, like it took a tranquilizer or meditated deeply for an hour.

"Some kind of large deer. Not a whitetail. I don't think I've ever seen one like this before," Father says.

"There is no debris," I say.

"From a car? No. I think an animal did this. Or animals. Coyotes, maybe. I've heard of bears nearby, but not quite this close to the city."

"Wolves?" I say.

"No. There are no wolves here. Not for miles."

"Something found its One," I say.

"Yes dear. Most certainly. Something found its One. Let's honor them."

I bow my head. I'm never sure what exactly to do in these moments. Father looks solemn. Mother never seems to bat an eye. She is far less sentimental. I look at my shoes and it occurs to me that I am stepping in blood. No matter.

*

Yuliana is six feet and two inches tall, a full foot taller than me. She went through a phase someway through elementary school, before I knew her, before I attended real school, when her mother enforced a hairstyle reminiscent of the starlets of 1980s music videos. The mother imposed this on Yuliana by waking her at 6:30 every morning and dragging her to the bathroom, bathing her in the bathtub, and applying volumizing product so that her hair rose an extra two inches above her scalp, and expanded downward. Conan the Barbarian with a pink and green fanny pack was the description she used. I had to look up who that was. Then I saw, and I was impressed by Yuliana's wit. That was one of the first days we spoke, in grade nine. I never met her mother. Her mother is dead. Her father is married to a new woman.

We sat together, that first day we met, in mostly silence, at the table where no one else sat. I remember feeling content. I had been worried about mistreatment; miraculously, they left us alone.

"Do you want to hear a song?" she asked me. I was eating a rib sandwich, which I only say with such certainty because I almost always ate the rib sandwich. I had been taking quarters from Father's van over the years, saving them for some unknown emergency. Then I discovered my school's rib sandwich, and the emergency became this sandwich's absence in my life.

"Alright," I said.

She pulled from her bag the world's smallest guitar. It looked like a toy. Maybe a couple feet in length. She finger-picked the most somber tunes. The instrument was quiet but I could hear it perfectly. Sideward glances came our way. People in the cafeteria turned their glazed faces toward us. Faces unknowing of anything. They watched her fingers from yards away.

Until I had met Yuliana, I never considered another person's One. Another person other than Mother, Father, and me, that is. You must never talk about it with anyone but your father and me, Mother reminds me regularly.

She strummed those tiny strings with such clairvoyance that I assumed she'd already dispatched her One. It was a matter of confidence. A purpose-driven life. I haven't yet asked Mother or Father about what happens when one must discover a new purpose.

*

I'll scorch the earth to find you

*

Mother enters my room while I am supposed to be doing my homework, but I can see through the reflection of my computer screen that it is clear to her that I am not currently doing homework. One look at the screen wouldn't necessarily confirm this, as the document I have opened is the essay I am supposed to be writing about climate change and what we as young individuals can do to prevent the destruction it will wreak upon us. But I can see that Mother can see that my attention is fixed to the buds in my ear and the distractions to which I am listening, not the page in front of me.

"What are you listening to?"

"A podcast."

Mother approaches and lifts one of the earbuds out of my ear.

"I understand that. What podcast is it?"

"It's about the benefits of living a purpose-driven life."

She yanks the headphones out of the computer. She

does not confiscate them like she did when I was younger. She affords me a false sense of autonomy. She places the headphones on the desk.

"It makes me unhappy seeing you listening to that sort of thing."

"I'm sorry."

"Don't apologize. Just don't do it."

"I will focus, Mother."

I turn to my computer and pretend to focus. Mother stands over me; I can feel her watching the screen.

"Climate change," she says, "is overblown fear mongering. Don't get wrapped up in the things people say just because they are popular."

"I know," I say. I have an urge to ask her about why she, a biologist, could feel this way. I have been feeling like questioning her more and more lately. This is a new feeling. It is exhilarating, even if I know that I will never do it. There's a thrill just in the thought of it. I decide I do not want to attempt to do my homework with her standing over me, and I turn to her.

"Tell me about your One again," I say.

"Lily," Mother says, blushing. "Focus on your work."

"I need a break," I say.

"You know we shouldn't talk about these things," she says.

"I know. Just the abridged version," I say.

"There is only one version," she says. This means she's going to talk.

"I was twenty," she says. "He was a year or two older than me. This was before I knew your father. I thought we were close, this man and I. Then he tried something,

something that was wrong. Very wrong. It became clear, almost right away. I knew within less than a day that he was my One. I knew within hours. Maybe minutes."

"How did you do it?"

Mother looks down at me. She strokes my hair. The only time she ever shows affection is when I ask her to speak about her One.

"I used a knife," she says.

"Where?"

"No. That's enough. We don't speak about these things. You have homework to do."

"Don't I need to know about these things? For myself?"

"Do your homework," Mother says.

"Why hasn't Father found his yet? What if it's too late?"

"Do your homework," Mother says, exiting the room. "And turn those podcasts off. Dinner will be ready in less than an hour. I want your homework done by then."

"It's going to take longer than an hour," I say.

Mother stares at me. I immediately regret talking back to her. Her eyes look a certain way. I turn to my computer and she leaves the room.

*

Father opens the trunk when we arrive at Ash's Mound. There is wind, minimal though it is, more than was predicted by my circling back to the weather app on Father's phone every thirty minutes, one of my tasks on Father-Lily Sundays at Ash's Mound. Father lets me unearth the cargo all on my own. I insert the key into the near-invisible slot in the right hand corner on the bed of the van's trunk. This loosens the mock carpet, which I lift on my own, despite its heft, and I fold it over completely so it rests like a rolled up Persian rug that could conceal a body. I insert the second key into the slot on the opposite side, and the spare tire and the black floor which surrounds it loosen, and I struggle this time but still manage to excavate the whole panel until it is halfway up, which is when Father's electronic rigging takes over automatically, and the floor rises robotically. Father asks me what I want to use today, the AR-15 or the HK91 .308.

"What about the others?" I say. I had assumed we were working with shotguns today. We have worked on assault rifles for weeks now. I have been craving the grip of Father's Mossberg. It is so wonderfully accustomed to my awkward little hands. I have finally learned its recoil well enough to shoot it confidently. But today is not the day, it would seem.

"We're not there yet," he says.

I point at the HK, which is a much more sophisticated challenge than the toy that is the AR-15. The AR's reputation alone has made me disdain it. A child can use it. Many have. It's a collective shame I want no part of. As I point, I think to myself, I am still a child.

"Shut up, Lily," I say out loud.

"Hey," Father says. "Be nice to my daughter." He touches the back of my head.

I look around. Horseshoe Mountain is perfectly clear in the distance. It is a lovely day. There are five new scarecrows set up in our field. Father must have come out here earlier in the week and set them up. Maybe we did them last time. I can't remember. I turn the keys and close the floor bed, and Father carries the HK. We walk to our spot in the breeze.

*

I am hellfire, raining down upon the impure

*

I do a solo run in the sewers in our neighborhood. Father spent years building tunnels that stretch from our basement into the tunnel system of the sewers on our street. He has never allowed me to do tunnel runs on my own. I've never thought about what the consequence might be if he caught me. I had been in the basement, looking for an old record in his collection, when the eerie, hollow wails unnerved me. It's a difficult sound to get used to. I went to slam the camouflaged tunnel door shut. I slammed and slammed, but it kept reopening. I let it open and stared. The blackness was inviting. I hadn't expected the feeling. I put on my rubber boots. I didn't bother with nose plugs. I have been used to the smells for years.

On my solo run I get lost twice and have to talk myself down from panicking. I have no map or navigation device. The flashlight strapped to my head is flickering. I want to make it back to the house. I picture myself starving to death and my body scavenged by rats. I think, if I walk in a straight line from where I am, I will come to the fake manhole cover in front of the Buffmeir's house. One

159

night, two years ago, Father replaced a manhole cover in our neighborhood with a fake. It's much lighter than a real one, and any person could lift it easily. No one would know who put it there if city workers ever discovered it.

I sit in the dark, counting my breaths. I know where I am. I know where I am. I know. Where. I am. I say it slowly. If I came this far, somewhere in my mind I know the way back, even if it all works the same. I will not die in the dark.

*

Yuliana tells me she is playing a show at the Corrigan and Crow Bar and asks if I would like to come. I ask her why a concert would take place in a bar and she assures me that this is a perfectly normal venue for such a performance. I ask her how we will be allowed into a bar at our age and she says she lied about her age and is in the process of getting a fake ID. This may work reasonably well for her, as, at her height and her mature look, she may just be convincing enough as a twenty-one-year-old, but there isn't the slightest chance that I will pass. I still look like a baby. I tell her this, and Yuliana assures me that I will be allowed in.

Convincing Mother and Father that I should go to a concert is a tricky affair. Surely I do not tell them it's being hosted in a bar. I wait. I wait and wait and wait. I do my homework with extreme diligence, so much so that I could even say that I've applied myself more than usual as far as Mother and Father are concerned. No easy feat. Ever since they stopped homeschooling me, it has been very difficult to assure them of my hard work, even if my grades are perfect. I did my usual chores, but I also vacuumed and cleaned all three bathrooms in the house over the course of two days. I did so conspicuously enough that they would notice I did these chores but wouldn't feel that I was rubbing the deeds in their faces. Mother says nothing, which is exactly what I want.

On Friday, with Yuliana here for a scheduled get-together, we play cards in the living room while Mother and Father prepare dinner. They are making enchiladas, which they still believe are my favorite food, but truth be told I have no favorite food. I find all food relatively enjoyable on an equal plane, with many, many exceptions. But Yuliana loves enchiladas, at least she claimed as such the first time she had them, which was here.

My plan is to ask about the concert at the dinner table. It is one thing to raise such an issue just the three of us, two on one. But, with Yuliana here, more than capable of arguing her points cleanly, not only are we two on two, but, more importantly, Mother and Father will see the source itself. The talent. It will be her concert. Even Mother will be at a loss for how to deny someone of something so close to their heart, that their best friend would be disallowed from attending her performance. It is as good a plan as we could hatch.

Mother and Father appear to be arguing about something. They are doing so at speaking volume, but I can interpret it well enough to be a disagreement. I cannot hear the words.

"Go fish," Yuliana says. "Can we play chess? This game is boring."

"Okay," I say.

I investigate the large cabinet in the den, which is where I believe the chessboard to be. I look slowly, and listen. Yuliana sings softly. Mother says She's losing focus every day. Father says You never say a word about focus to me. Mother says You're forty-six, you've been training for years, I'm not worried about you. You'll find yours when it happens. That's not what I'm talking about. Father says She trains just fine. If you came with us, even just on our runs, just once, you'd see that. She outpaces me. Mother says Don't be cute with me about this. You know I don't need to train like you or her. Frankly, I think it's ridiculous that you bring that up. Father says Don't start with the hip again. Mother says Are you joking? You're being completely unfair. For three weeks I was in a hospital bed. I struggle to remember what you did when he ran that red... what was it? Oh that's right! You dodged out of the way. You ran away from me. Father says We're here again? How many times can we go revisit this? Yuliana keeps singing. Mother says You ran. So don't tell me anything about why I don't come running with you. She needs focus. Father says She is focused. There's a pause and Father says Just admit to me, for once, that you resent me because I haven't found mine yet. Well, it's mine. My One. My choice. My life. It's my One. Yuliana stops singing. Mother says That is completely nuts and I'll never admit that because it is one hundred percent not true.

I return to the coffee table with the chessboard and we set up. Yuliana is white and I am black. She makes her move and we get going. She is very good, which I attribute to her half-Russian heritage, and though I know that to reduce things to nationality is simplistic and often flawed, about fifteen moves into our game I remember when she first mentioned that her extremely Russian father taught her how to play, so I feel validated to be thinking in stereotypes, yet annoyed that I didn't initially remember it. Ten minutes in and I have her mostly crippled; queenless, one rook, one bishop, one knight. I have all my pieces minus a rook and two pawns. But she is still dangerous. She's only ever mated me three times, but one of those wins she managed without a queen. It's her move when she looks at me and leans in close. She whispers, "What's a One?"

"A what?" I say.

"A One? My One, he said? What does that mean?" she whispers.

I make my move and stare at the board. I look up, and see she is looking right at me.

"I have no idea," I say.

*

Father and I set up fifty meters away from the centre scarecrow. He has the backpack; he hands me the rifle and I deal with it. He takes off the bag and takes out the blanket. He doesn't roll it out yet, just leaves it in a heap. He takes out a tripod but I don't think we'll use it. He hands me the magazine and I load it. He reaches in and a bunch of money falls out of the bag. It must be a thousand dollars, maybe more.

"What's that for?" I say.

"This is savings. When I bought the crossbow last

week, he gave me a huge discount. I guess I forgot to put the money away. Never you mind about that. Focus!"

"Auto or semi?" I say. He scoffs and does a very fake dad laugh. I flip it to semi-automatic.

"Did you bring a scope?" I ask.

"Hey, sweetheart, if you keep talking like that your mother and I are going to make you eat nothing but boiled celery for a week," he says.

I point the rifle and he says, "Hawk."

I squeeze a single round and the center scarecrow's pumpkin-head explodes.

He says "Vulture," and I pivot, squeeze one round, miss, squeeze another and the head of the farthest left scarecrow explodes.

He says "Eagle," and I pivot, and squeeze one round and the head of the second from the right explodes.

He says "Hummingbird," and I pivot, squeeze one round, miss, squeeze another round, and miss. I must get visibly exasperated because Father almost right away says, "Hey, hey. Just breathe. Don't worry about it. Breathe." I lift the gun. I squeeze. Head explodes.

He says "Albatross," I pivot, squeeze one round, and hit the last remaining scarecrow in the sternum. I lower the gun. Father is looking at me. I turn to face him.

"Waiting for something?" he says. I just stare at Father. I smirk, I think. I probably look very dorky when I try to smirk. I never smirk. There's a snapping sound in the distance, the sound of wood breaking. The scarecrow topples over, broken in two.

"Not anymore," I say.

"Look at Wild Bill Cool Girl with the one-liners," he

says. "He was still standing and you let him stay standing. That's a miss. But since he's ruined now, you won't be able to score that one. Four out of five."

"Come on," I say.

"That's not very impressive, sweetheart."

"I was accurate."

"Four out of five," he says.

"I made it completely snap in half! How is that not accurate?"

"It's not just about accuracy. Four out of five."

He jogs toward the scarecrows to replace exploded pumpkin heads. I suppose things will be scored out of four from now on. Father is crafty, maybe he'll build a new one. I put the rifle on the ground and take Father's knife out of his bag. I can see Father assessing the damage on the fallen scarecrow.

"I'm so sure you were aiming for that," I hear him say.

*

I am a collector of severed heads

*

Yuliana's concert is immensely fun. It is the most fun I can remember having in three years. Every band is unique from the next. Yuliana performs second out of five bands. The first band is some kind of hardcore punk group and people are moving into each other violently for the duration of the set. Then Yuliana takes to the stage by herself, and the looks around the audience are mostly of confusion. People must have been expecting more of the same. Yuliana plays her little guitar and sings in her somber voice for twenty-two minutes. Maybe for the first two minutes there are snickers, yawns, wandering eyes. But everyone is paying attention within three. A boy buys me a beer. I hate it. I take one sip and spit it out. He tells me not to be a baby and I stare at him until he walks away.

Outside a group of us sit on the curb while people compliment and fawn over Yuliana. They smoke cigarettes. I try one and also hate it, but I don't cough. One of the men from the second last band seems quite taken with Yuliana. She takes sips from his flask. He must be twice her age. He has long hair and a beard. But I can't tell if she likes him back. She may only be entertaining him for the use of his flask.

Yuliana pulls me into her and holds me close in a way that she has never done before. It feels motherly. I find it very strange. It makes the bearded man back off.

While we are all outside, breaking noise laws and drinking while underage and doing things that Mother and Father would lock me in the cellar for, Yuliana asks if I want to come to her family's cabin in a few weeks.

"It's in California," she says, "Far north. Really bare bones. There's basically nothing there but evergreen trees and mountains and bears and mountain lions. It's the most perfect place on earth."

I tell her I'll ask, but I know without a doubt that Mother and Father would never say yes. It would be impossible.

"I didn't know Russians had cottages in California," a boy says. I had thought the same thing but didn't say it.

"It's my grandfather's. On my mom's side," she says. "You fly to Reno. Then you drive two and a half, three hours west, through the desert, into the mountains."

"Can I come?" the boy says.

"No. Piss off." She speaks into my ear. "You need to get away from your parents for a change."

No one has ever said that to me.

"I don't think they would approve," I say.

"We'll tell them it's a field trip."

"I really don't know if that's going to work," I say.

"You managed to get yourself here, didn't you?" she says.

*

This is my world. I will set it on fire and find you in the ashes

*

On the drive home, I turn to Father and say, "You're not going to tell Mother, are you?"

"About what?" he says.

"The four out of five."

Father keeps driving without talking for a full thirty seconds before he says, "What are you worried about that for? She's not taking you out here. I am."

"I know you keep her informed of my progress."

"Well, she is your mother after all."

"She's going to be mad."

Father looks at me. "What am I? Chopped liver?"

"It's not that," I tell him. "It's just... she's mean about it. You're always nice. Calm. I don't want to deal with her sometimes."

Father pulls the van over, nearly running over a skunk in the process.

"Listen to me," he says. "Everything your mother and I do for you, we do together. We are a team, the three of us. How many families are there like us, that are this close?"

"I don't know," I say.

"None, that's how many. We lead a purpose-driven life."

"She's done hers."

"Look at me. Look at me, Lily. We are all in this together. If your mother is hard on you, it's the same thing as me being hard on you. We want you to be ready, to succeed. That's what it's all about. Understand?"

"Yes."

I do not, in fact, understand. I'm sick of talking about it.

We drive for some time. Mountains pass by like background ornaments. It occurs to me that Father and I haven't done a mountain run in a few months. We have been more focused on strength lately, which I quite enjoy.

"I have a question," I say.

"Yes, dear?"

"If a person commits suicide, does that mean that they decided that they are their own One?"

Father doesn't answer right away, and I'm not sure if it's because he's avoiding the question or because he's thinking.

"No," he eventually says.

"How come?"

"I... I don't really know. It just isn't," he says.

"But why?"

"Because a person can't be their own One. They just... they just can't. The One must, uh, be external."

"But... why?"

"I don't make the rules, sweetheart."

"But – "

"No," he says.

When we get home, Father jogs upstairs to put his backpack away. I follow quietly and watch him. He unloads his backpack on the bed. He removes the knife and puts it in a drawer in his desk. He removes the first-aid kit and sticks it in the closet. He removes the bundle of cash from the side pocket of the bag and puts it in his little shoebox in the closet. He doesn't know that I'm watching him. He sees me watching him and smiles.

"What are you looking at?" he says. He pushes the shoebox into the shadows of the closet and closes the door.

"I have a question to ask you," I say.

"Ask away," he says.

"I think you might say yes. But I'm worried Mother will say no. It's for a school field trip."

*

I am the end of all things

*

The plane lands in San Francisco, and Yuliana and

I have to run as fast as we can to the gate to catch our next flight, which leaves in twenty minutes. We get stuck in a line for a security checkpoint. I compulsively check my watch every fifteen seconds while Yuliana whistles to herself. They open a new line, and we manage to squeeze through with five minutes left. We run with our bags, clunkily and slow, like salmon trying to flap out of water toward a grizzly's mouth.

Mother insisted I be reachable the entire time, so she purchased a cellular phone for me. She also insisted on speaking with the teacher that would be chaperoning us before we left. I told her Mrs. Mukherjee would be happy to speak to her on the phone, hoping Mother wouldn't insist on a meeting. I asked why Yuliana chose the name Mrs. Mukherjee, and she said it was because we have a civics teacher with that actual name, which I didn't know, and because her friend Tatiana can do an immaculate adult Bengali accent.

The flight to Reno is so bumpy that the man behind us throws up. We hear it happening. The child beside him would have been my choice for the likelier victim of turbulence. This was only my second flight ever. When the man throws up, I feel a little tiny splash on the exposed part of my heel.

The plane lands in Reno and we wait a half hour for Yuliana's aunt's boyfriend to arrive. In the meantime, I call Mother to pre-emptively assuage her anxieties. There is no answer so I leave a message. I do not like having a portable phone with me. I feel handcuffed by it.

Our chauffeur arrives. He drives a red, rusting two-door hatchback, the back floor of which is riddled with empty beer cans. He has long, curly black hair and I can't understand what he says when he speaks. His name is Bob Nelson, and he insists that we use both names. Yuliana sits in the back with me while Bob Nelson drives 100 miles per hour through the desert while drinking beer as he drives. He chain-smokes cigarettes and I become covered in ash after only a short time. The ride is bumpy, like the flight. He offers us beers for the drive. Yuliana drinks one. She hands it to me but I wave it away.

The drive would be lovely if I didn't spend it fearing for my life. I know that life is both fleeting and meaningless without the meaning I assign it through the pursuit of my One, but in the moment where death looms close, it becomes difficult to imagine anything to do with purpose and all I feel is the impulse to live.

We arrive at the cabin three hours after we left the airport, and Yuliana's Aunt Maggie runs out of the cabin like a dog and practically tackles her much taller niece with a hug. Maggie has an open bottle of alcohol in her hand but manages to not spill a drop. We are surrounded by pine trees and sunshine and buzzing wasps and an ambient smell of wood smoke. Maggie then hugs me with almost as much enthusiasm as she had hugged Yuliana.

She brings us inside, carrying most of our bags herself, despite the bottle in her hand. She pours a glass of tequila for Yuliana. The cabin is small. There is a funny smell, something musky, that is almost unpleasant but it is barely acceptable. The wooden walls in the little great room look like they would fall apart if a strong enough wind blew across the mountains. The fridge is upside down.

"Why is the fridge upside down?" is the first thing I say since I've been here.

"She needs time to recharge, hun. Flip her over and she finds her way. Takes a good day. You're dry!" Maggie hands me a plastic cup filled with clear liquid. I don't seem to have a choice in the matter. I'm told it's tequila. I take a minuscule sip. There is an elderly man outside, looking out over the valley behind the house. We all go outside.

"Grandpa!" Yuliana says. The old man waves with the back of his hand but says nothing. He is looking at something through binoculars. The back of the cabin overlooks an immense valley, and far in the distance are mountains. They look different from the Rockies I'm used to. Less tall, but more alive. More proximate. Grandpa is looking down into the valley with his binoculars.

"He might be a while. Became obsessed with the new lion cubs," Maggie says. I seem to have left my tequila inside.

"Did you say lion?" Yuliana says.

"Mountain lions!" Maggie says. "Mama had two cubs! They live down there. All he does is look at them"

"Where is the father?" I ask.

"They never stick around too long," Maggie says.

There's an array of red, cheap-looking chairs made of a kind of loose fabric. They seem like the type of things people might associate with camping. Father and I have never sat in such chairs during any of our excursions. I sit in one and am immediately overcome with a feeling of comfort I've never felt before.

Yuliana runs up to her grandfather and puts her arm around him. For a moment it seems he has no ability to perceive that another human is touching him. He eventually acknowledges Yuliana by handing her the binoculars. She looks and then exclaims as if she sees the lions.

"Wanna beer?" Bob Nelson says to me, sitting on the ground next to my chair.

"No, thank you," I say.

"Okay. Wanna smoke a joint?" he says.

"No thank you."

"Well Christ! What do you want then?" he says.

"May I have a glass of water?"

Bob Nelson gets up without speaking. He emerges from the cabin three minutes later with a plastic cup filled with a translucent liquid that I hope is not water. I will spend the next few days dehydrated. Neither Mother nor Father would approve.

Yuliana's grandfather eventually removes himself from his vantage point and joins us. He says very little, and when he does speak his voice is quiet and he speaks slowly, like a film at half speed. I can't hear him very well so I pretend and nod at whatever he says. Bob Nelson hands him a beer, which he proceeds to drink almost entirely in one gulp.

"He wants wine!" Maggie says.

"But he drank the beer," Bob Nelson says.

"But he wants wine! He told me earlier he wanted wine!" Maggie says.

"But he drank the beer," Bob Nelson says.

"That. Lion. Really. Loves. Her. Cubs," Grandpa says.

"How can you tell?" Yuliana says.

"Ohhhhhh. It's quite clear," Grandpa says. He gets up and walks around the cabin, out of sight.

"Can you believe he's eighty-seven? He's still publishing!" Maggie says.

"Publishing?" I say.

"He's a world-famous linguistics professor!" Maggie says.

"World famous," Bob Nelson says mockingly. Maggie looks at him like she will end his life before morning. My heart skips a beat for reasons I can't quite identify. I look at Bob Nelson. He doesn't look back at me, but I can feel that he feels my look.

Grandpa returns with a pile of wood in his arms that looks far too heavy for a man his size and age.

"Look at that ox!" Maggie says. Grandpa dumps the wood in the firepit, and then begins assembling it into a castle of logs.

"There's no ban?" Yuliana says.

"Of course there is. He doesn't care," Maggie says. Grandpa waves his hand.

"There's been a ban all season. Fires up by Crestville are real bad. Evacuations. Highway 3's been shut for weeks. It's bad," Bob Nelson says.

"It's bad," Maggie mimics him. "It's bad. It's bad."

"Why do you keep saying that?" he says.

"Because it's obviously bad! It's fucked! If there's evacuations, it's not just bad, it's fucked! It's redundant! Redundant! Stupid!" Maggie says. She storms off. Bob Nelson watches her go back into the cabin.

After the fire is built, Bob Nelson and Grandpa cook steaks on a small charcoal grill, while Maggie, Yuliana, and

I make a salad and prepare mashed potatoes. I am bored, so after ten minutes of peeling potatoes I go outside and join the men by the grill. There are dozens of wasps buzzing around. Neither Bob Nelson nor Grandpa seem to care. One lands on Bob Nelson's shoulder and I think it stings him. He barely reacts. The smell of smoke, between the grill and the ambient smoke in the air from the nearby fires, is overwhelming. My eyes are watering and I think I am lightheaded, but everyone here is weathered by this environment and I don't want to be thought of as a baby, so I ignore it as best I can. I check my phone, surprised that Mother has not called back, and I see that I have no bars of reception. I go into the cabin.

"How do I get reception for my phone here?" I ask Yuliana.

"Oh, honey, there's no reception up here. Not for like thirty miles," Maggie says. Yuliana does not look at me and continues to wash Romaine lettuce. I feel a sense of discomfort in my chest I have never felt before. My face becomes flush. I go back outside and a wasp nearly flies into my mouth. I go right back inside and say, "How do I get reception? I need to have reception. My mother insisted on being able to reach me and we told her she could."

"I mean, we can go into town tomorrow. Although I think we were going to hike tomorrow. Maybe Sunday? We'll be on the mountains all day," Maggie says. Yuliana continues to assemble the salad. She looks at the spinning lettuce with ridiculous, unnecessary focus.

Dinner is delicious, but I don't enjoy it because I am very nervous and my throat feels like it's closing up. My heart is racing. It will be four days until I speak to Mother. I drink a glass of wine. Bob Nelson and Maggie argue about which is the tallest mountain in the national park we will be visiting tomorrow. Grandpa lets the argument continue, and then when there is finally quiet he confirms which mountain is highest. Yuliana talks about her music. Maggie insists that she sing something and Yuliana promises she will later. Maggie refills my wine glass even though it is not empty. I notice a rifle hanging on the wall. I am shocked I hadn't noticed it earlier. I stare at it while the conversation happens around me. Someone asks me what my hobbies are. I say firearms without thinking. Bob Nelson perks up and attempts to talk to me about guns. Grandpa joins the conversation. I can't really hear what they are saying or can't focus because now I've had more wine and I feel blurry but things feel more nice and laughy and my heart isn't racing as much.

We sit by a fire, with sounds of crickets, and no wasps, and Bob Nelson plays a little guitar while Yuliana sings. Yuliana sits beside me and hugs me as she sings. I feel uncomfortable in her arms.

We sleep in the bed in the little attic alcove of the cabin. It's late and I hear Bob Nelson and Maggie arguing for a long time. Bob Nelson was prohibited from driving home to his cabin because he drank too much. Yuliana is snoring. I check my phone to see if the reception has magically come back. I nudge Yuliana. She shifts and continues to snore. Maggie accuses Bob Nelson of being a drunk. Bob Nelson looks for a word that I believe is hypocrite, can't find it, and then tells Maggie that she drinks more than him. I shove Yuliana and she snorts and wakes up.

"What happened?" she says.

"You knew I wouldn't have reception up here," I whisper.

"What? What time is it?" she says.

"You knew, before we came. You didn't tell me, on purpose. You didn't want my parents to reach me."

"Do you really think it would be more fun here with them breathing down your neck every hour?" she says. "Come on." She moves as if she's going to do something and I await to feel her putting an arm around me but she doesn't do it. "Trust me. They won't kill you. So you'll be grounded for like a month. You'll tell them the phone didn't work. She bought it for you after all. It can be her fault. I promise, this won't be a big deal."

I don't sleep. The sun rises before seven and I get out of bed shortly after dawn and go outside to breathe the air. It's still smoky, but less so. I can hear Bob Nelson snoring from another room. Grandpa is already outside, standing in his spot, watching the lions. I approach him, and before being able to say anything he waves with the back of his hand. He holds out the binoculars, and I take them and look. He helps me aim them and I see the lion licking one of her cubs. There looks to be a small pile of bones and maybe a skull of some kind beside the lions.

"I. Think. That. Was. A. Young. Deer," Grandpa says.

I stand watching with him for over an hour.

We eat eggs and bacon for breakfast. Bob Nelson is not at the table, but I no longer hear snoring. His car is gone. I stare at the rifle on the wall as we eat. I was expecting to be more nervous this morning about the lack of phone reception, but I care less than I assumed I would.

We hike up a mountain, Yuliana, Grandpa, Maggie, and myself. It is over 12,000 feet in elevation. The hike is easy for me. I keep well ahead of the others. Then we hike another mountain that is nearly 15,000 feet in elevation. Yuliana moves slowly. She says, during a rest, that she's done it before, but had forgotten how hard the altitude hits her. She and Maggie end up falling behind. Grandpa tries to keep pace with me, but I pull ahead. He stops me and hands me a huge bowie knife in a sheath of black leather. I pull the knife out and look at the gleam in the blade. He says that I should have it just in case. I ask just in case of what? He says Lions. I say Don't you need it? He rolls up his sleeve and flexes his nonexistent bicep. I get to the top of the mountain a full half hour before Grandpa, and a full hour before Maggie and Yuliana. They are wheezing and pouring sweat when they reach the top. While I wait for them, I sit under a boulder and look at the knife. The eight-inch blade is thick and razor sharp. I contemplate the notion that her elderly grandfather carries this thing in case he runs into a mountain lion. It seems like a foregone conclusion, what would happen in that instance. I check my phone, because perhaps up here I have reception. It's not in my pocket. I left it beside the bed.

*

I'll scorch the earth to find you

*

We arrive at the Denver airport Tuesday afternoon. I check my phone and there is no indication that anyone has called. On the drive back to the Reno airport I had reception but there were no calls. I was too scared to call. Yuliana slept with her head on my shoulder during that drive just as she slept with her head on my shoulder during the flight. Her head was heavy and dug in like a drill, but I didn't move it. I didn't sleep a wink. Bob Nelson had driven us to the Reno airport. He smoked and drank beers the whole way. The dust of the desert stung my face and dried my eyes and throat. It didn't bother me. If he crashed or we died in a sandstorm, I wouldn't have to face Mother.

A strange thing happens at the Denver airport, once we have landed and deplaned. We are supposed to be picked up by Yuliana's parents. When neither of them is there, Yuliana calls. She has a quick conversation, during which she says very little even though she's on the line for about four minutes, at the end of which she looks like she has seen a ghost. After she hangs up, she says, "They're coming. Just a little delayed."

"Tell it to me straight," I say. "How dead am I?"

"My stepmom said something happened. She said it in this kinda way. I don't know. I think something's wrong," she says.

I look into her eyes. I know she's lying to me. The trap has been set. Yuliana is now complicit in my ultimate grounding. She is the gravedigger.

"Why aren't they here yet?" I say.

"My dad's on the way. He got delayed. I don't know," she says. She's nervous and sweating.

"Do you have any money left on you?" I say.

"Why?"

"I'm hungry and my blood sugar is very low. I don't want to faint. I should get a sandwich."

Yuliana reaches into her bag and pulls out a twenty.

"Do you want anything?" I say. She shakes her head and then decides better of it. She hands me two fives and says, "That should be enough. Get me whatever. No pork," she says.

I take the cash and my knapsack and shuffle through the crowded terminal. I find an exit on the other side, and find the taxi sign.

*

The cab rolls through my neighborhood, and still, no one has called my cell phone. We are at the end of my street, about four hundred feet away from the house, when I notice police tape. I tell the driver to stop. Neither Mother nor Father's cars are in the driveway. I notice the police car, just the one. It is parked, and an officer is sitting in the driver's seat, looking bored. The tape surrounds the house.

"Miss?" the driver says.

I give him the thirty dollars, ten more than the meter says.

"Oh, thank you very much! Thank you!" he says as I leave. I close the door quietly.

I stand in the middle of the road. He drives away. I look at the police car, the tape, the bored officer.

I am fifty feet from the Buffmeirs' house.

I walk over to the manhole cover. It is light as a feather. A red car drives by, a woman in the driver's seat. I close the manhole back over my head just to catch her expression as she sees me, her little neighbor, dumping myself into a sewer.

I use the dim light of the cell phone to light my way. I can't see much in front of me. Even though it is a straight line to my house, the tunnels don't work that way. I have to turn right farther down the street, then left, well past my house, then left again, and then again. 500 paces, 200, 300, 200. I figure it out myself, just like when I was down here by myself, weeks ago. I still must have reception down here because Yuliana calls. I do not answer.

I realize now, my feet and lower legs soaking in sewage water, that this decision might be idiotic. I considered the options quickly. If the police are waiting for me because I ran away from the airport, then likely there isn't more than one. The house must be empty. I will be quick. I will be silent. I will pack a bag and then leave. It occurs to me that it is not very likely that running away from Yuliana at the airport would yield such a response, but if it's something worse, I don't want to know. I will pack a bag, and I will leave. Just leave. Somewhere.

I come in through the tunnels, through the basement. I come up to the kitchen and stand. All the windows are closed. The curtains drawn. I've never heard the house this quiet. I creep through the kitchen and the living room. Empty.

I go upstairs and put my bag on my bed. I unpack it and throw everything in my laundry hamper. Some of my clothes are covered in twigs and sand and I make a small mess on my carpet. I sit on the bed, thinking about how much trouble I'm in. Mother will pull me out of school. I nearly laughed when Yuliana suggested I'd be grounded. I don't quite understand how I could let her put me in this position. I feel betrayed. I cry for a few seconds before breathing deeply and forcing myself to stop. My nose leaks mucus and I'm sure I look ridiculous. I look out the window. The one police car sits there. I wouldn't have thought anything of it if it weren't for the police tape. My phone rings. Yuliana again. I don't answer it. I sit there for some time. Then I hear sirens. I look outside, and the police car has left. I hope I did not benefit from someone else's tragedy.

I go downstairs. The house is a mess. The dinner table has plates and glasses on it. In the kitchen, the mess is worse. There are dirty dishes all over; evidence of a meal that was cooked but not cleaned up. I've never seen this kind of disorder in my house. I know I am supposed to be hungry, but my stomach is in knots. I open the fridge and there isn't much there. I pour myself a glass of chocolate milk. I drink it in three gulps and my stomach feels worse.

I turn on the TV. The couch feels uncomfortable. I scroll through channels, not really paying attention. I don't want to leave. Where would I go? I desperately want to leave. I can go anywhere. I sit with my indecision.

I don't want to watch anything. It's the middle of the afternoon, so nothing much is on. I leave the TV on a fishing show for three minutes and then I keep flipping. I return to the kitchen and look through the fridge again. I don't see anything I want. I stand staring at the mess. On one of the plates beside the sink is an earwig. I look at it. The pincers on its backside lurk like devil horns. The earwig crawls off the plate and into the sink.

I sit back down on the couch and resume flipping channels. In a flash I see my father's face. I backtrack three channels to CNN and there he is, Father. His face, in the top right corner. I try to listen to what's being said but I can't hear anything. My ears seem as if they are packed with gauze. The man reading the news has no voice. The picture of my father looks a few years old and must be the most unflattering, most serious-looking photo of him that exists. A photo I've never seen. The news anchor says that since the shooting yesterday, investigators have been baffled that he was, as far as everyone who knew him is concerned, a normal family man. He says something about my mother. Something about questions.

I use the house phone and call Mother's work number. There is no answer. The news anchor says that they have yet to establish a motive as to why my father shot the woman. I sit on the floor. I very much want to turn off the TV but I can't. They show a picture of the woman. She has blonde hair. She is maybe ten years younger than Mother and in the picture is wearing a university graduation robe. Then the news anchor says something about the five officers that were shot. I call Mother again.

There are interviews. Witnesses. After Father shot the woman, he waited in the back of the van for the police to arrive. A witness on the TV, who is crying, and for some reason I am convinced is fake-crying, says all she can recall is how much blood there was on the street. The news anchor confirms that the fifth officer that was shot died in the hospital. A witness says something about seeing a piece of brain on the ground. I can't believe that was actually said. Did I imagine it? I pictured it. I think I imagined it. Father's picture is back on the TV.

I call Father's work phone. There is no answer. Then I hear the part on the TV I was waiting for. That after Father shot the fifth officer, he was shot. That he is now dead. A witness says thank god no one else was hurt. Thank god they managed to take him down. A witness says bless those officers who gave their lives. They died brave, defending our country from another deranged psychopath.

I watch until it gets dark. I look outside for more police cars but none come. I stop calling Mother. I don't think she is at work. The president speaks about the incident in a press conference. People speak about gun violence. About gun control. About something called homegrown terrorism. I worry that they will show an image of father's body. I dread seeing that. But I can't turn it off. It occurs to me that this is irrational. Would they show that? They might. I don't know.

I call Yuliana's house. She answers. I say nothing but she knows it's me. She starts crying.

"You should come here," she says. "Stay here with us. I'll get my stepmom to come get – ," she doesn't finish her sentence as there is yelling in the background, her father I think. "My dad is mad you didn't wait. He's gonna come pick you up. Are you at home?"

I hang up.

It's dark. Late. 10 P.M. I'm alone. The phone rings. I answer it and it is Mother.

"Lily. Thank god you're home. How did you get in

the house? Are you with the police?"

"No," I say. "They're gone."

"I want you to listen to me very carefully. Are you listening?" she says.

"Yes."

"I want you to pack a bag, right now. I will be home in half an hour. You and I are going somewhere. We will be gone from home for some time," she says.

"Where are we going?" I say.

"I want you to pack a bag with clothes and be ready for me. Do you understand?" she says.

"Yes."

"I will be home in half an hour."

"Where are we going?"

"Away."

"What about the police?" I say.

She hangs up. I sit, listening to a police chief talk about fallen officers in the line of duty. There's a long segment about the lives of one of the officers who my father killed yesterday. He was a veteran and an occasional volunteer at an animal shelter in Fort Collins.

I go upstairs and pack a bag, the same bag I brought to the cabin. I don't think much about the items I select. I stuff them in, letting them come unfolded. I run into my parents' room and go into the walk-in closet. I find the white shoebox where Father keeps his extra money. I take a large handful of hundred-dollar bills and stuff it into my pocket. There is a piece of crumpled paper in the shoebox that catches my eye, because it is the only item that is not money. I uncrumple it and read what looks like some sort of poem.

I am a god of war
I am an angel of death
I'll scorch the earth to find you
I am hellfire, raining down on the impure
I am a collector of severed heads
This is my world. I will set it on fire and find you in
the ashes
I am the end of all things
I'll scorch the earth to find you

It's written in Father's handwriting. I put it in my pocket. I start crying. It pours out. I cannot stop.

"Stop," I say to myself. I must focus. I rock back and forth.

"Stop. Stop." I regain some composure and then I quickly remove the poem from my pocket. It feels extremely icky to touch the paper, like something horrible, like earwigs all over my skin, and I throw it on the floor. I kick it into the shadows of the closet.

I call a taxi; I remember that the taxi that we took back from the airport had the number on the door, an easy number, one to remember; 222-3422. I ask for a taxi to take me to the airport. I tell them it's urgent.

*

Mother has been calling my cell phone all day. I ask the taxi driver, about a half an hour outside of Reno, if he can lower the window, as he has the child locks on and I can't do it myself. He says it will be very dusty and windy. I say it is just for a second. He lowers it and I throw the cell phone out the window.

"Did you just litter?" he says.

"No."

"I ain't getting a ticket for littering on account of you. This is already an out-of-ordinary length drive. I stay in the city. I'm doing a big favor here. Don't be littering when you're in my car, understand?"

I nod yes. I don't know if he sees me. After an hour of driving, he asks me about my red eyes. I say I'm fine. He hands me a tissue.

He drops me off somewhere near the cabin. It's a heavily wooded road and I can't remember the address. I walk for two hours, in the heat and dense smoke, until I find the road that is familiar to me. The smoke is much thicker than it was just two days before.

I find the dirt road to the cabin. I walk down the long driveway. The front door is unlocked, but I knock. Yuliana's grandpa comes to the door.

"Oh. Hello."

"Hi," I say.

"What. Are. You. Doing. Here?"

"I... My flight was canceled. And I really like it here. Can I stay here for a few days?" Grandpa looks around, as if someone could be watching. He looks at his watch. He seems confused.

"Do. Your. Parents. Know. You're. Here?"

"Yes. They understand. Yuliana got on a different flight."

He looks uncertain of what to do, but he lets me in. I sit on the couch. I see his binoculars on the table. I am very thirsty, but I don't want to ask for anything. Grandpa is standing not far from me, contemplating things. He says we should go into town soon and make the appropriate phone calls. I ask if it's alright if I just stay here. He doesn't respond. He walks away, into his bedroom. I think back to my cab ride here and wonder, did I really throw my cell phone out the window? I reach into my pocket and it's still there.

I am in Mother's car, in the passenger seat. We drive in silence. I feel my cell phone in my pocket. We have been driving for nearly two hours. I have asked twice where we are going, but Mother remains silent. The route is unfamiliar to me. I thought I knew virtually every road in and out of Denver for dozens of miles, given all the climbs and excursions Father and I do together. Father.

My bag is in the trunk. I can hear it sliding around. The thought that hurts my head is whether Mother has guns in the car like Father. I don't believe she does, but of course it is possible. Perhaps if she did, she would have gotten rid of them.

"What about school?" I say.

"We'll find you a new one," she says.

"Why are we leaving?" I say. "This is because of Father? What he did? Are we in trouble?"

"No," Mother says.

"He never found his One," I say.

Mother looks at me. She looks furious. "What are you talking about?" she says.

"Only One. You said it can only be One. You both said it. He did six."

Mother drives with her face forward, but I can feel she's searching for the right thing to say.

"He had his reasons," is all she can muster.

"No! You said it can only be One! He's a fake! Liar! You're both liars!"

Mother raises her hand and I shield myself. No hands come down on me. We continue to drive and Mother wipes small tears away, even though she is trying to hide it.

We pull into a gas station. Mother fills up the car while I sit in silence. There's a pickup truck beside us with a California license plate. There are four of them, three boys and one girl, all a few years older than me. They seem carefree. One has dreadlocks. There is a surfboard in the bed of the trunk. One of them sees me staring at them and waves at me. I don't wave back but I want to.

Mother tells me she is going in to pay, to get us sandwiches, and to use the washroom. I stare at the surfers. Everything about them is light, free. They probably live precariously, maybe like nomads, but they appear to be in very high spirits. They are a different kind of human than I am. I lower the window. I believe that if I ask them to take me with them, wherever it is they are going, there is a chance they will say yes. I look towards the front door of the gas station and still see no sign of Mother. I look back to the truck. The surfers are all looking at me now. They can feel me watching them.

"Hey," the girl says. I stick my head out the window.

"Hi," I say.

Grandpa says that we must evacuate the cabin. There is now an emergency fire advisory for the area, and the forest fires may strike as soon as five or six hours from now. He says we can try to drive into town, but the roads will close soon, so we must hurry. They may already be closed. I sit at the table, eating the turkey sandwich that he has prepared for me. I stare at the rifle on the wall. Grandpa says that he's going to use the washroom, and then we must leave. I nod.

If he takes me into town, he will surely call home. All this will be over. I'll be forced to go back.

Once we're driving again, Mother asks me who those young people were. I say I don't know. She says that I spoke to them so I must know who they were. I'm not hungry, but I bite into my turkey sandwich so she won't bother me about it.

"They were surfers," I say.

"Do they know who you are? Did you tell them anything about yourself? About us?" Mother says.

I just shake my head. I can see in the side-view mirror that the truck is behind us. Perhaps they'll follow us and stop at the next place where we stop. There's still time. There's still time to ask for them to take me with them. It's still possible. In front of us are fields. Endless fields. Rockies pockmark the horizon. I could climb a mountain. Even if they don't stop where we stop, when we stop next, I could run. Into the fields. Up a mountain. I could run. Mother is not fit. She would never catch me. I could run into a field and never come back.

Grandpa goes to use the washroom, and immediately I get up and approach the rifle on the wall. It's too high for me to reach so I push a chair up to the wall and stand on the chair. I try to take it down, but the rifle is locked in place and I don't have a key. I descend. I pace around the cabin. I notice, resting on the table near the front door, is Grandpa's sheathed bowie knife. I pick it up. I clip the sheath onto my shorts. I exit the cabin out the back door. The smoke is thick and my eyes burn. I stand on the spot where Grandpa normally stands. I look down, but it's too difficult to tell if they are there from this distance. I make my descent. Down into the valley. It is rocky and steep, so I must be careful, but Father and I have done worse descents than this. I slip and scrape my knee. It stops me for a few minutes, as the initial scrape is quite painful. Then I continue. Down, down into that huge valley, into the river. I'm up to my thighs in water. The water is freezing, refreshing. The smoke is slightly better down here. I creep, very slowly, and then step inadvertently into a deep spot. My head is submerged underneath. I emerge, as slowly as possible, just so my head peaks above the water. I see them. They are there, in their spot. The mother is resting while the cubs wrestle. I watch them, mostly submerged. The mother smells the air. Why haven't they left? The fires will devour them. I hold the grip of the knife under the water. Slowly, as slowly as I can, I surface. First just my shoulders. Father taught me how to move like water in water, how not to make a sound. I emerge, and the mother sees me. I emerge, knife in hand. The mother is standing, but the cubs are oblivious. The mother growls at me. I stare at her. She approaches, one step, another step, wound tight as death, her teeth bared. Her fangs are dripping. I take a step toward her. I feel the knife in my hand. It is an extension of me. The mother growls, and arches her back. I hold the knife firmly in my hand. Smoke fills my eyes.

Neon

I remember the first time I saw someone die at Neon. There would be another. His name was Conn Henderson. He was a tower of a man, who looked like Elton John if Elton John had been a linebacker. Even in his old age (I pegged him at somewhere around 70) he was still an immense figure. He wore elaborate, multicolored designer suits, and always came in with a matching hat. On the night I saw him die, his hat had a long feather in it. It looked as if it could have been a quill. I never asked what he did for a living; the quill made me think he might have been a writer. A particularly successful and eccentric one, that is. Maybe all the successful ones turn out to be eccentric. But then again, his name wasn't familiar to me outside of his previous visits to Neon. He always dined alone, except on his last night, when he was with another man, younger than him, but not by too much.

I remember he picked up the jellied cube on his plate and inspected it as if looking through a magnifying lens to examine a diamond for flaws. I had told him and his guest, when I dropped the plate in front of them with the two perfect, square-inch cubes, that they would learn what it was after the following course, as both courses were meant to coincide. His guest ate the cube first, and reacted positively, though subdued compared to what I expected. Conn then plucked his cube with chopsticks and placed it into his mouth like a dental hygienist inserting a suction tube. I watched his eyes go wide. We knew, from his profile, he had no allergies. He chewed slowly, appearing deeply affected by the experience. After he finally swallowed the morsel, he stood up and declared in his mighty basso, "It's perfect! It's perfect! The taste! That's it! That's the taste! Mother!" The whole room froze. All guests at Neon eat the same courses at the same time, but no one had quite reacted so expressively. Then he winced; he grabbed his chest and collapsed into his chair, clearly in distress. His friend helped him lie on the floor. I stood against the wall, and watched. Other staff jumped into the scene to help, but I couldn't move. His breathing continued to intensify. The other guests in the small room stood by as someone called an ambulance. It didn't arrive in time.

I remember the first time Chef Le Main called me by my name. When I first started, he usually called me Bitch, if anything at all. But that became confusing because he also referred to Rachel as Bitch. She was much taller than me, so he switched my name to Short Bitch. I still had long hair at the time, otherwise I'm sure he would have called me Bald Bitch, or something like that. Everyone had such nicknames. Darnell was Blacky. April was Month. One day he called me Barbarella. I didn't understand why, but I certainly preferred it to Short Bitch. It stuck for roughly a week. Then one day out of the blue he called me Nifty. I didn't assume that he had known my name the whole time; he must have asked someone. There was a girl that worked in the kitchen here for a month, to whom he referred exclusively as Faggot. One day she became upset, and began crying while reducing some rhubarb liqueur gelée before clarifying it, not because of Chef's insults, but because earlier that day she had learned that her mother had been diagnosed with breast cancer. She took off her cook's hat, in a moment of exasperation, inadvertently letting her hair down, and Chef said, "My god! You're a girl? Ha! I had no idea." He still called her Faggot until she stopped working there.

I remember the first time Sophie showed me the wires. She'd been cagey the whole day, and before the beginning of service she pulled me aside and showed me the gash in her arm. She'd cut herself on a jagged piece of metal on the walk-in fridge, after Chef Le Main had to hammer the door open when he lost his key. The cut was deep, and she had kept it duct-taped and hidden under her sleeve. She showed it to me because she was worried. I looked in the wound and saw an assortment of grey, yellow, and chrome wires. "Isn't it cool?" she said. I told her I thought it was very interesting.

I remember the dining room at Neon. To call it a dining room is disingenuous. To call this disingenuous is putting it too mildly. Dining room is something you picture in a house, where mother, father, son, and daughter sit and eat roasted beef and mashed potatoes and green beans while discussing their days. Son avoids questions about what he learned. Daughter excuses herself early because her boyfriend is on his way to take her out. Mother drinks more wine than she should to mask the fact that she hates father. Father wades in his own impotent, invented context of power. This thing that we call the dining room, it doesn't belong in the terminology of what we really do. But if it must be the default, nowhere was the term more a betrayal of truth than at Neon. It was an art gallery and a dungeon. A chamber of wonders. A dreamscape. It was small. Two long tables. All guests, never more than 20, sat together for one seating. Nothing brings strangers together like sharing the planet's most ambitious culinary experiments. The scents inside the room fluctuated as the meal progressed, tuned perfectly to guide the guest toward the next course. But nothing stood out more than the lights. Pulsating hypnotic colors. The endless luminant buzz, the enveloping warmth. I dream in neon, in purple, in electric night. Natural sun is an assault, Chef said. The room had no windows, regardless of where we were in the city. Every week, service moved to a new, secret location. And every week, the room was the same. The relocation efforts alone required a whole massive staff, but the rest of us still took part. I remember moving slabs; waking up at 4 AM to ride with the trucks; kitchens changed, but Chef adjusted with mind-boggling efficiency. Mise en quel place? The colors, I never quite got used to them. No one did. Maybe that was the point.

I remember James. Or Jamie. Boy or girl? I seem to have trouble remembering that detail, and I can't understand why. I wish I could explain myself. He or she started working there shortly before me. He was a starer.

She would lock eyes with me and wouldn't avert the gaze before me. It was unnerving. The eyes were undeniable, gorgeous, almost inhuman. Especially in that room. Did he/she have long hair or short? Breasts? Delicate, thin arms, or bulging biceps? I don't remember. But I remember the eyes with every fiber of my memory. I think of them when I need to feel warm and safe. Chef watched her look at me. Chef watched me look back at him, at James. Jamie. Identity unclear. Will confirm sooner or later. Chef caught those glances every time.

I remember the night the Polish soccer star Tomas Berenholz came to Neon. He had tears in his eyes the entire meal. His wife rubbed his back while he chewed and cried. It became a more somber evening than we were used to. When I cleared the second to last dessert course, he held my arm. He told me that his grandfather escaped Poland just as the Nazis had invaded. His parents and three sisters were never to be seen again. He traveled east and made it to the Russian border, where the soviet army interrogated him and accused him of being a Nazi spy, so they imprisoned him in Siberia for two years, in the Gulag. He watched every friend he made starve to death over the course of those two years. He told me that his grandfather never spoke about this experience, except for one night when he got drunk at a family gathering and recounted his most memorable moment from his time in the Gulag. A cat wandered into his cell that night. It was mangy and skittish, with gray-white fur and whiskers on only the right side of its face. It saddled up beside him. Tomas reiterated to me that this was his grandfather's most memorable moment because, that night, he was able to eat a real meal. Tomas cried while telling this story, still holding my arm, as his wife rubbed his back, and said in broken English, "Zaida ate stray cat so I can eat the best meal on this planet earth." His face glowed purple, and the tears that streamed down his cheeks appeared dyed the color of setting suns. At the end of the night, once the guests were gone, I told Chef Le Main the story. He took a very serious look, and said he would include stray cat on the menu one day.

I remember, when I was younger, we lived in a seaside beach town, the name of which escapes me. The sun was always setting or close to setting. At least that's how I remember it. The horizon was always pink-orange. The temperature was always perfect. We ran on the beach. We had no troubles. I think of this place often.

I remember there were no rules in the dining room at Neon. Guests could smoke, take drugs, or act lewd in whatever ways they felt like. Most people maintained decorum and acted reasonably, probably because they were in awe of their surroundings and were willing to relinquish power to the otherworldly legend, Chef Le Main. But not all deferred. A drug dealer waited until course five or six, when people were already halfway drunk, and began selling cocaine to guests. They partook right in the moment. This proved disastrous for the meal, as their appetites were ruined, so Chef Le Main adjusted as best he could. Everything came out of the kitchen in liquid form. The guests drank their meals, formerly enervated faces now manic with delight and frenzy, until they could drink no more. Chef spoke to the dealer privately, and told him next time to bring weed, not coke. I remember once a man smoked a gargantuan cigar throughout the entire meal, filling the dining room with thick, acrid smoke. The room could not assert itself, sensorially, the way it should. Chef Le Main adjusted, changing the menu in real time as best he could. We were all confused. We didn't know our drop lines. Course seven came out. The cigar-smoking man chortled through each bite, smoke blossoming out of his mouth and nose, sharing space in his cavities with the masticated morsels. By the time course eight came out, he had excused himself. He tried to eat course nine, but returned to the bathroom again. I told Chef. He simply shrugged his shoulders, and gave the subtlest of winks. As I left the kitchen he said, "Maybe you should snub out his cigar. He may not be back."

I remember the time James or Jamie didn't show up for work for two weeks. I asked people if they knew where he was, but no one did. I found reactions to my question confusing, and even in some cases unsettling. They all said things like, "Oh, I hadn't really noticed she was gone." I asked Chef Le Main, but he told me never to ask questions regarding front of house staffing, which I found odd because he was the Chef that I had worked for in my life that tended to have the most interest in his front-of-house staff. Then, like nothing had happened, Jamie and James were back. I asked them where they went. They said they had taken time off. I was so relieved to be able to look in her blue eyes again.

I remember when the terminally ill artist Anastasia Pelon brought her whole family to Neon for one last dinner together. We had been expecting a room full of eccentricity, full of chaos, full of the infusions that such a prominent artist would have inevitably left on her closest family members, especially in the shadow of her imminent death. But what we got was something much different; a room full of working-class, down-to-earth, polite people, who all happened to be this woman's family. There was never an unsmiling face around the room. These parents, siblings, and cousins were so happy to be together. Anastasia's sister helped her whenever she needed to use the bathroom or stretch her legs. Her sister would carry her oxygen tank as they walked together, holding each other's arm. I remember the expectation that the whimsical and ferocious aesthetic that imbued her art would reveal itself in the room, but no. The bloody, bodily, confrontational, qualities of her work had no role here. There was only love. Between the last savory course and the first dessert course, a brief pause came to the service and a projector was wheeled in, so that the family could share memories. The pictures showed them together at various times in their life. We were all withdrawn, mournful. But they, the family, were so full of life and hope, despite their impending loss. Near the end of the final course Anastasia became ghostly white. She grabbed her chest, and her breathing shortened. Everyone at the table stood up, panicked. Her father shouted, "This is it!" Her sister held her, attempting to lie her down, and Anastasia began laughing. She laughed so hard that chunks of Mille-Feuille flew out of her mouth. Family members laughed and sighed, as did we. "You people just make it so easy," Anastasia said, coughing. James/Jamie watched the family leave the restaurant, thanking us and Chef, elated, already grieving. We held each other's hands as tightly as we could. We thought of our own families. Jamie/James didn't say this, but I imagined them saying, "This is our family now."

I remember the woman with the swan. She wore it on her head like a hat. We'd seen animals in here, live ones. The swan appeared stuffed, but something about it felt very much alive. She said, "If that slobbering popcorn pixie Bjork can wear one as a dress for the Oscars, I can wear a real one on my head. Eat your heart out, Norway, or wherever." People laughed. Her husband said, "Dear, everyone knows Bjork's from Iceland." I couldn't help myself, and said, "She's eaten here, you know." The swan atop this grey-haired woman's head may not have moved all night, but I could have sworn that it was looking at me. Every time I entered the dining room, I felt its eyes digging into me. I asked James/Jamie if they felt it too. They said yes, they certainly did.

I remember wondering if I had wires. I remember contemplating whether I should look.

I remember the room, after what must have been my fortieth week, beginning to feel like a cave, like a dungeon from which there was no escape. The lack of natural light was affecting us. Our moods were becoming erratic. People tended not to leave their job at Neon; it was too prestigious. People left Neon all the time; it was too high-pressure. I spoke to Jamie and James about the increasingly unnerving feeling that the walls were caving in. They both felt the same way.

I remember having a disagreement with Chef about something. Something trivial. What exactly, I don't recall. During the argument, he stopped referring to me as Nifty and resumed calling me Bitch. I said to him, "Don't talk to me like that." He looked stunned, beside himself. "What did you say?" he asked, not sarcastically. He was genuinely unsure if he heard right. I said, "I said don't talk to me like that." He swallowed hard. He appeared as if something dreadful had happened. He left the kitchen.

I remember all-you-can-eat caviar night. Chef decided impulsively that the first course after the amuse bouches would involve an indefinite sequence of 250-gram tins of Beluga caviar, served family style, with blini, and vintage Krug. If a tin of caviar was finished, the guests were not to be asked if they wanted more; a new tin was to be brought immediately. If a champagne glass was empty, it was to be refilled. Only when all twenty guests in the dining room agreed that they were done were we to move on. When we told chef that the restaurant would lose thousands of dollars in the execution of this plan, he threw his cleaver at the wall and told us not to question him. He said he was in the mood for excess. James or Jamie and I agreed, Chef may have been starting to lose his sense of reality. Our guests that night happened to be particularly excessive, and particularly hungry. 26 tins of caviar, 16 bottles of Krug, and 2 hours later, we progressed. It was nearly 10 P.M. when we cleared away the last of the empty tins, some still lined with scatterings of tiny black pearls. Guests were spilling, slouching, screaming, laughing. A glass broke. Then another. We slipped in seamlessly, of course, to remove any evidence of disorder or destruction, but still, this felt different, as if things might be unraveling. I could see Chef popping his head into the dining room from time to time. He had never done that before. Sure, he would come in and speak to guests here and there, famous actors, hedge fund managers, princes, and models that insisted on complimenting him personally, but on those occasions his presence was always deliberate. This was different.

I remember that night vividly because it was the night that James and Jamie and I decided we would leave Neon. Sure, we were in the middle of Asia, in Singapore, a city where we had no other connections. But we agreed it was time. And it had to be together. We needed each other. James/Jamie said that he/she would come to work one day soon with a shaved head, and that would be the signal, the last shift, the moment we would walk out together. The word I kept wanting to use, every time I spoke to this person, whose face is now a grey static fuzz, was escape. I retreated to a bathroom near the end of service, at nearly three in the morning, with a fish-filleting knife I stole from a cook, and I put the blade to my hair. But, somehow, Chef must have found out about our plan. Because the next night, when I arrived at the restaurant, ready for the coup, there was no one there except Chef. He took me into the kitchen and told me service had been called off for the evening. His meat cleaver sat a few feet away from him, from us, on the prep table. Its presence was ominous, especially given that everything else was spotless. There were no other knives or plates or items of any kind lying around. Just the cleaver. I asked him why service was canceled and he said, "Because certain things had to happen." He looked me in the eyes. And I understood. "Nifty," he said. "You're the best we could ever have. The best. There's never been anyone better." I understood. I nodded my acknowledgment. He took me by the arm and led me to a little closet just outside the kitchen. He opened it, showing me the mess inside. Liquids and parts. A disembodied smile. Wires. "You see?" he said. I nodded. "Had to happen," he said. "No choice at all." I nodded. He put his hand on my shoulder. "Things must stay the way they are. That's how we make everything function." I nodded. I stared at the mess in front of me.

I remember sitting in the empty dining room, with the regular lights on, the walls black. I remember thinking, this is my home. This is my home. This sunless box. I didn't know the time. I tried to relish in the solitude, to breathe it in, but the walls always felt as if they were edging closer and closer, and soon enough I would be crushed. I pictured the ocean. I pictured the trees. I pictured my seaside childhood town. I could almost smell the salt water. I closed my eyes and imagined the ocean.

It's getting dark now. I should probably turn in.

I've made a decision. Tomorrow I will look inside myself, and see if I have the wires. If I do, maybe I will show them to a guest. I haven't decided yet.

Chef would be very mad at me if I did that. But something inside me has changed. I can't explain it. Something in me... I don't feel the urge to serve anymore. Maybe something good will happen.

Reasons to Stay

It's been 11 months since your last response   You
climb the eavestrough. It's raining. My keys are on my
desk, my roommate knocked out on cold meds. You're
soaked, scaling my outside wall like a squirrel. I watch,
drenched, too afraid to try. You slide my window open.
Thirty seconds later you're letting me into my own
building, blonde hair dripping, glasses fogged   I
consider excuses to message you. You borrowed a book
when we dated. Can't remember which one. I pick
a random title, knowing it's wrong   Before our
first date I slice my thumb at work, on wine foil. We go
bowling, your idea. My first roll I bleed on the lane, slip,
crack my head. The rest of the date is at my place, you
monitoring my concussion   You say you don't
use Facebook, or whatever, naked on my bed. I say I
want to snoop pictures of you. You say I'll have to take
them myself   You mention the diagnosis casually.
Once it's over you'll practice law again, but not at a firm

After some casual texting, the first time in years, you tell me you got into law school. I'm happy for you, if you're happy   I tell you, on our second date, that I've applied to international PhD programs, there's a chance I might move away   We first meet because you sit at my bar, awaiting a job interview, a job you don't get. I pour you water even though you decline it. I miss, spilling on the bar, your lap   I scour the internet, looking for traces of you, hints you're still alive   You don't take your glasses off during sex because you wouldn't be able to see anything, and you say you want to see me   You tell me you've never traveled. I spend our fourth date encouraging travel in all forms, like I've been to exotic places. I've never been outside the country. Before you ask, I tell you I got accepted into a program, and will move away at the end of the summer   We make friendly small talk. I ask what you've been up to, planning to suggest we go for coffee. You ask if I finished my PhD. "No, and I've decided not to continue. I'm back home." I don't suggest we meet, and then you tell me that, to be honest, things have been tough, because you're in treatment for cancer   We go rock climbing. You're a natural, just like when you climbed into my apartment. I'm stunned by how strong you are. I ask what sports you played in college. You say you've never worked out a day in your life   You tell me you weigh less than 100 pounds, from the chemo and the bowel obstruction. You tell me this as a warning, for when we see each other, which we've agreed to do, one last time. I ask how something like this can happen to someone so young. You reply with a "shrugging" emoji You tell me you want to end things, even though last week you thought you were fine to keep dating until I left. I say "ok." A month later I message if we can have coffee, just friends. You say "sure!" We meet at the subway. We fuck three times that night. We agree to continue dating, for as long as we can   After I've been at school for a semester, you ask why we didn't try long distance, say that you would have been willing   You call me the day before we're to meet, tell me you've changed your mind. It's too hard, in this terminal state. I don't tell you I'm devastated I won't see you. We text throughout the day. I ask, "How long?" Two to six months. Palliative bed is in the house now. Your tone on the phone has been sad, but now you say you're euphoric. Feelings fluctuate radically. At the moment, you feel free. These are the last texts I receive from you. The next day   I never hear word, officially. At first, I assume you've chosen to end this newfound correspondence, because you find it too hard. I keep messaging you. I wonder what I've done wrong. I fear the worst. There's nothing online. No obituary. No updates. I don't know your family. Those few members whose social mediamedias I find haven't posted in years. I can't find photos of you, any evidence you existed, except the images in my head. These blocks, fragments, in whatever order they come   At your place, during a record heatwave, we lie on top of the sheets, naked, fans blowing, proud of ourselves. You say you feel this should be the last time we see each other, to give the hurt of my upcoming departure some cushion. I say "Ok." Two days later you call, ask if I want to take a trip to a national park, go hiking. I say "Ok". It pours the whole time and we build our tent in the rain. You laugh at my ineptitude, my waterlogged grumpiness. You do the bulk of the hard work. You wring water from your shirt onto my face while I nap, and keel over laughing at my thrashing. We watch a brown bear scratch its back against a tree, and then stumble and roll down a hill. You attempt to follow the bear but I stop you. The bear runs off when it sees you staring at it. I rip a hole in the tent when I slip while peeing outside and grip the thing out of panic. You use scotch tape to patch it. We sleep with an impromptu skylight. The sky is clear and we see outer space through our tent hole. "Look at all that dazzling shit out there," you say. You lie on my chest. I don't remember sleeping that night. You lie awake too, I think. I don't remember   I remember.

ACKNOWLEDGEMENTS

Thank you to Emma Lindquist. Your love and support mean the world to me. You've always championed my work, made sure I had time and freedom to write. You've always made me feel that I should be doing this. I would not be writing if it weren't for you.

Thank you to Jon Nix at With an X for all your great care and consideration in publishing this collection, and to Cris Crude for the wicked cover design.

Thank you to Sarah Dipoce for your lifelong commitment to putting me in my place.

Thank you to Michelle Isocianu for helping me carve out some of the aesthetic details in these stories and in the tone and curation of the collection.

Thank you to Tarek Ghader, Ariel Fisher, Madsie Boufard, Ryan Davis, Jeff Goodman, Jonathan Football Rubinoss, Mike Coffey, Anna Press, Chris Zeischegg, Charlene Elsby, David Kuhnlein, Claire Hopple, Sara Lippmann Thomas Moore, Amanda Rico, Sztella Muzslai, Ben Wannamaker, Julia Monson, Juan Valencia, Tyler Barney, Kieran Meyn, and the friends and readers that have given me ideas, words, feedback, and artwork on these stories.

Thank you to Anthony Rose, Kari Maaren, Alex Moore, Jeremy Andriano, Melissa Fox, the Thursday Group, that now meets on Mondays. Special thank you to Mark Lovewell for bringing me into the group all those years ago and for nearly two decades of mentorship. Thank you to Jen Frankel, Bobbi Speck, Helen Walsh, Inya Ivkovic, Candi Pugh, and anyone who has passed through the group over the years and told me not to be so goddamn quiet all the time, not to beat readers to death, shit like that.

Thank you to Mallory Smart, Talia Blatt, Ben Drevlow, Jason Teal, Micaela Brinsley, Eponine Howarth, Ignacio Oliden, The Librarians of the Internet Void, Alban Fischer, Anita Levin, Sandra Fluck, Scott Garson, and the editorial teams at the journals that first published some of these stories.

Thank you to Rachel Skipper-Horton for somehow connecting with me, just before the end.

Included stories have previously appeared in:

Container - Maudlin House

Bird Eating Glass - The Harvard Advocate

Does Anyone Care How the Vegetable Oil Feels - BULL

Progress - Heavy Feather Review

Rhino - La Piccioleta Barca

Elevator Etiquette - The Free Library of the Internet Void

Length - TRNSFR, Sip Cup

Headwalking - HASH Journal

Scorch Earth - The Write Launch

Reasons To Stay - Wigleaf

About the Author

Derek Fisher is a writer from Toronto. He is the author of Night Life (Posthuman Magazine, 2023). He's had work published in Maudlin House, X-R-A-Y, Wigleaf, The Harvard Advocate, Fugitives & Futurists, Heavy Feather Review, Tragickal, BULL, Atlas & Alice, and more. To see more of his writing, visit derekafisher.com

WITH AN